Other books by Deirdre Hutchins

**The Paranormal Investigators League series**

PIL #1  Voodoo in Savannah

PIL #2  A Hanging in Tucson

PIL #3  Suicide on Sunset

PIL #4  The Legend of Providence

PIL #5  Darkness in Denver

PIL Prequel: The Origin Story

**The Dark Prophecy trilogy**

1: Resurrection of the Vampire

2: Vengeance of the Damned

3: Deliverance from the Prophecy


These are all available from the San Joaquin Valley Press.


Visit us at www.sanjoaquinvalleypress.com

Daphne Winters Psychic Investigation Series
#1

# The Body and the Soul

A Novel

By Deirdre Hutchins

San Joaquin Valley Press
Fresno, California

*The Body and the Soul* is published by
San Joaquin Valley Press
P.O. Box 9485
Fresno, CA  93792
www.sanjoaquinvalleypress.com



Cover design by Andria Davis Kaye
The cover is a collage of elements from Shutterstock: Ghostly girl by Gromovataya, Lake by ggcarrle, Bloodstains by Nik Merkulov

We are grateful to Tracy Olivar Tafoya for answering a few technical questions.

ISBN 978-1-7378061-6-5

# PROLOGUE

I could hear the water before I saw it, coming out of the woods.  I was surrounded by trees, thick and low hanging.  Birds chirped all around me to show their happiness at the blessing of another day.  The sun was barely beginning to fill the earth with its light and warmth.  But the sound of the water called me.

Why was I out here in the woods by the lake?

I pushed through the branches effortlessly.  And, as if in a trance, I walked toward the water—both curious and slightly hesitant at the thought of what I might find.  Although I couldn't rationalize the reason, I just knew the water had a story to tell.  One I might need to hear.

Lap, lap.  The water bobbed and splashed rhythmically along the shoreline.  I kept advancing.

A sound to my right caught my attention: thump, thump.  I turned my head slightly, not wanting to completely lose my focus on the water before me, but curious about the noise.  I saw a woman out for her morning jog.  She had a good stride, was a good runner.  And the morning was perfect for a run by the lake.

She slowed when she neared me, and at first I assumed it was because she didn't want to run into me.  But then I noticed she was *following* me.  She advanced as slowly as I toward the water's edge.  Was the lapping sound of the water a siren's call to us both?

No, there was something in the water.

It bobbed on the surface in a way that made it blend into its surroundings, but it was still so apparent that it shouldn't be there.  And a part of me didn't want to know what it was.  A part of me was afraid of what it might be.  But the other part of me, the part that kept advancing, *had* to know.

It was the bone-chilling scream from the jogger that woke me from my trance and gave me a tunnel of clarity.  It wasn't just a random foreign object floating on the water.  It was a human body.  And even more frightening was the absolute certainty with which I knew whose body it was the instant the woman screamed.

The young girl bobbing in the water, face down, with her blonde hair fanning out in every direction, was *me*.

# 1.

Detective Miguel Alvarez sipped his black coffee from a Styrofoam cup. He rubbed his eyes and willed his body to get energized and ready for the day. He loved building a case for the prosecution—the absolute satisfaction of putting the "bad guy" behind bars—but still this line of work took its toll. Every once in a while he thought jealously about people who had chosen to be veterinarians or teachers, working with the innocence of animals and children.

"You look like shit." His partner, Gina, sat down at the desk across from his, placing her feet up on her desk. The Sarge hated when she did that, which was ninety percent of the reason why she did it.

"Just living the dream."  Miguel forced himself to sit up straight and type his credentials into his computer. He knew that, other than the bags under his eyes, he looked well put together.  Miguel rarely left the house without ensuring every hair was gelled perfectly in place. "Did you finish the reports on Mack?"

Gina rolled her eyes.  "Don't worry.  We built an airtight case.  That asshole is going to prison for a very long time."

"Everything needs to be perfect.  I don't want any cracks or loopholes for the defense," Miguel said again. He tried to just seem like a good cop, but the worry lines told a different story.

Gina lowered her feet and then leaned in toward her desk so she didn't have to talk loud.  "Mack isn't a rich, white man in power like Denton.  You did your job, Mikey. I did mine.  We're good."

Miguel nodded but the certainty didn't move past the gesture.  He was plagued with doubts, that some little technicality would undo the months they'd spent on the hunt, gathering the evidence, talking to witnesses.  No matter how many times he did this, and he got better every time, it still felt like there was some legal mumbo jumbo that he hadn't sealed the lid on.  Like Denton.  Miguel and Gina had both been furious when the crime lord got off on a technicality.  After years of investigation and compiling evidence.

When had justice become a game?

"Alvarez!" Minnie called from the front.  "A lady on line two says she has important info for your case."

Miguel looked at Gina, who raised an eyebrow in response.  "Put her through," he instructed Minnie, then quickly lifted the desk phone when line two lit up.  "Detective Alvarez."

A bold woman's voice came through the line. "Hi.  Detective Mike Alvarez, right?"

"Speaking."  Miguel locked eyes with Gina.  She was intrigued as she watched the scene before her unfold.

"Oh good.  I have information for you for your

case on Grace Collins," the woman said.

"Grace Collins? I don't have a case on Grace Collins."  Miguel shrugged at Gina and his partner instantly began searching their database for the name.

"You will.  I'm positive it will be your case," the woman said. "She was murdered last night."

"Did you see it happen?" Miguel asked slowly, not sure how to process this bizarre conversation.

"No," the woman replied.

"Then how, may I ask, do you know this information?" the detective asked just as Gina shook her head back at Miguel.

"Nothing in the database, no missing persons. Nothing on a Grace Collins," Gina told him with a frown.

"She told me," the woman said with a small sigh.

"I thought you said she was murdered?" Miguel asked, trying to piece it all together.

"Yes.  I'm a psychic medium and the spirit of Grace Collins is here in my living room with intricate details I think you'll be interested in," the woman said again.

Miguel hung his head for just a second.  He dealt with crazies all the time, but it never got any easier.  He had a full case load and the case against Mack to present to the District Attorney of Fresno.  He didn't have time for this.

"Ma'am, there is no Grace Collins even reported missing.  I'm sure you *think* you are talking to her ghost, but I assure you this is just a hallucination," Miguel explained slowly, assuming that the woman was likely on drugs.  Although she spoke clearly and purposefully like a confident woman, her words told a different story.

"Daphne Winters," the woman responded.  Her tone was so crisp it jarred him.

"Huh?"

"Not 'ma'am.'  My name is Daphne.  And I can assure *you* that the case of Grace Collins will hit your desk.  And when it does you need to call me," the woman explained and then ended the call.

Miguel held the phone in the air for a second

before hanging up.

"What was that all about?" Gina asked.

"Is it just me, or do the crazies get crazier and crazier every year?"

Gina laughed.  They *definitely* had their share of those in this line of work.

"I think we need to go after a warrant for that apartment on Clark Street," Gina said, referring to a case they'd been working for weeks.  She had been trying to get inside that apartment for a while now, certain that the smoking gun was there.  Miguel wasn't as convinced.

"We don't have enough yet.  You know Judge Bustamante will just throw it out," he said shaking his head.  "Let's go talk to the girlfriend.  I know she knows something."

Gina pointed at her partner.  "I'm getting in that apartment."

He held his hands up.  "I know.  We will.  But we have to do this right.  You know how it works."

Gina admired his attention to detail and, most of

all, his patience.  It's what made him so great at his job.  But Gina wasn't wired that way.  She was incredibly impatient.  She thought that perhaps their opposing styles were part of what made them such a great team.  She kept him from going too slow, and he kept her from rushing and being too sloppy.

"Fine. The girlfriend."  Gina stood and threw on her gray business jacket.  Her dark hair was pulled in a low ponytail and curled.  Her make-up was flawless, as always.  Gina felt it was critical to look feminine if she was going to compete with all the men around her in the Fresno P.D.  She was always dressed professionally and looking sharp.  Miguel didn't think he'd ever seen her in sweats with no make-up.  Couldn't even wrap his mind around it.

"I'll drive."  He grabbed his keys and shook them as he stood.

"Dork."  She shook her head, laughing at her partner.

"Alvarez!  Malone!" It was the Sarge.  He had a

stack of papers in his hands.  "I need you to head out to Millerton.  A jogger called in a young girl's body floating in the lake, and the Sheriff's Department needs a rep from Fresno P.D."

"Can't you send Johnson?  We've got a full caseload," Gina groaned.

"Besides, we're homicide detectives.  She could've simply drowned," Miguel added.  One more case was the last thing they needed right now.

"The slash across her throat says otherwise."  The Sarge frowned at them both.  "Looks like the crime happened before she was thrown in the lake, and her ID says Fresno, so Sheriff's Department needs one of us on the scene. And you two are up.  So quit your bitching and get a move on."

"We'll go check it out, get the details and then head to the girlfriend's house," Gina said to Miguel.  But he wasn't sure why his spine was tingling with the memory of the phone call with Daphne Winters earlier.

Something told him this wasn't going to be a

simple one.

And he hated to admit it, but a small voice inside his mind wondered if the girl floating in Millerton Lake with a slashed throat was Grace Collins.

But he said nothing to his partner as they hopped in the car and headed for Millerton Lake.

# 2.

Daphne Winters dried off from the shower and got dressed in a hurry.  She wasn't embarrassed to be naked in front of ghosts—she'd gotten over that a long time ago—but she was worried that at any moment Detective Alvarez would connect the dots and call.

She wasn't bothered by the detective's dismissal of her claims either.  It wasn't the first time she'd encountered a skeptic.  People who claimed to be logical were always resistant to the most logical thing right in front of them.

And Daphne was new here.

In Los Angeles, where she'd lived for many years, she'd built up a reputation with the police force as someone they could trust.  But here, in California's Central Valley, nobody knew her.  And she loved that. She would've been happy as a turtle dove not to talk to another homicide detective for the rest of her days, but the frightened blonde ghost in her bedroom watching her put an end to that.

And Daphne could ignore a lot of things.  She could ignore rudeness.  She was used to it.  Hell, she could be blunt and rude herself.  She could ignore the rich and arrogant.  She could ignore ignorance.

But the ghost of a young girl in need of someone's help?  Daphne had never been able to ignore that.

As a child, it hadn't taken her long to realize she was different.  People were judgmentally quick to tell her so.  The spirits that came to her regularly, night and day, weren't coming to her friends and family.  No one else could see them.  But Daphne had never really viewed it as a burden.

If she was the only one who could help them,

then that's what she'd do.

But it hadn't won her any personality awards. She was ostracized and branded as weird from the get-go. And Daphne quickly adapted to the role. How could she be anything but what she was? She'd never made friends easily, with the living anyway, and so she was very picky about who she considered to be one. Weird and quirky. And psychic. That was her and she was fine with that.

She towel-dried her short bleach-blonde hair, letting it go every which way and not giving one hairy shit. Her black T-shirt and her long, bohemian skirt completed her look. So far in Fresno, no one had given her any attitude for her quirks and she found herself wondering why she hadn't moved here years ago.

Her cell phone rang from her nightstand and she quickly ran from the bathroom to answer it. A quick check of the caller ID told her it was not Detective Alvarez. Normally she would've happily ignored anyone she wasn't expecting, but in this case it was a nice surprise.

"Duane," Daphne said as she answered.  A rare smile crossed her face.  She sat on the bed to continue the conversation. "To what do I owe this pleasure?"

"Hi, Daph," Duane said with a sigh.  He was never one for many words, so Daphne had to wonder why he'd called instead of texted.  Neither one of them was much of a talker.  "It's good to hear your voice."

Her heart squeezed a bit.  She'd loved Duane from the moment she'd laid eyes on his muscled physique and gorgeous baby blues.  And those feelings died hard.  Even if she was running from them somewhat. "And yours."

"We have a case.  Duncan thinks you'd be perfect for it.  It's in Philly," Duane explained.

Daphne shook her head.  Work.  It was always work. "I'm working a case right now."  She looked up and locked eyes with a frightened blonde ghost.

"Daph, come home.  We all miss you."  Duane's voice trailed off at the end.  "*I* miss you," he quickly added.  He wasn't big on public displays of affection, so Daphne knew this was a big deal.  He really did miss her.

"Duaney,"—Daphne spoke softly, her voice laced with emotion—"I miss you too, but you know I can't.  And honestly, I like it here."  She could say that with conviction because it was true.  Sure, she'd only been here a few months, but she was finding the fresh start to be just what she needed.

"Well, you know we'll always be your family, right?" Duane asked.  "And you can always come back to us."

She knew.  "Tell Duncan to set up cameras in the backyard."

"What?"

"For that case in Philly.  The ghost isn't haunting the house.  It's the land."

Duane laughed at her diversion tactic.  He knew her far too well.  "Will you ever forgive me?"

Daphne had to swallow the lump in her throat.  "There's nothing to forgive.  You are who you are and I love you for it.  And Duane?"

"Yeah?"

"I'm not running from you."  Well, maybe she was a little bit.  "I'm running from ghosts.  You understand?"

Duane was silent for a moment before he said, "Of course I do."  He did.  He'd spent most of his life obsessed with the supernatural and running from ghosts of his own.  "Don't be a stranger, Daph.  We need you."

Daphne waved a hand in front of her face even though he couldn't see it.  "Yeah, yeah.  You know I'll catch one of your little ghost-hunting expeditions one of these days."  And she meant it.  She couldn't cut ties with the Paranormal Investigators League completely.  They were the only family she had anymore.

"Bye, Daphne."

"Bye, Duane."  The call ended and Daphne looked at the digital clock on her nightstand.  Was nine in the morning too early for a glass of wine?

Duncan, the founder of the Paranormal

Investigators League she sometimes helped with cases, was one of the first people she'd ever met who accepted her. And Duane was one of his team members—one that Daphne had been attracted to from the get-go. After they'd gotten somewhat close on a case in Denver,[1] she and Duane had tried to make a go of it, but after a few dates, awkward for both of them, he'd called it quits.

The blonde ghost of Grace Collins appeared in front of her, standing at her bedside. Daphne wondered if maybe she could sense Daphne's emotions just as Daphne could sense hers. A part of Daphne had known from the beginning that it would never have worked out with Duane. They were both too much alike, if she was being honest with herself. It didn't stop her from trying. Again and again.

And it didn't stop it from breaking her heart.

"Men, huh?" she asked the ghost. In response, Grace just looked like she might cry. Complete anguish covered her face. Daphne realized she had likely been a

---

[1] You'll find the details in Deirdre's *Darkness in Denver*.

very pretty young girl.  When ghosts appeared to her, they usually looked however they'd died.  Car accident victims were mangled and bloody.  Heart attack victims were blue.  In Grace's case, her throat had been slashed and the front of her clothing was stained red from her own blood.  Her hair was mangled and ratted, sticks and twigs coming out of it.  She had bruises on her arms and face.  Someone had beaten this girl before they'd taken her life.

"I want you to tell me everything you know, Grace.  And I'll make sure whoever hurt you never does this to anyone else again," Daphne said.  The ghost of Grace nodded in response.  "Good.  Now start at the beginning."

# 3.

"Her name is Grace Collins," the Deputy from the Sheriff's Department on the scene explained as he caught Miguel and Gina up to speed.

Miguel and Gina exchanged a look.

"You have her ID?" Gina asked, curious how a homicide had been so tidy on details that were often elusive.

"She still had her purse around her neck," he answered.

"That's convenient," Miguel muttered. "Next of kin?"

The uniform nodded. "They're being notified now." He pointed to an area that was thick with trees.

"The jogger that found her is still here.  Pretty shaken up, but she gave her full statement."

"Thanks," Gina said, with her eyes on the jogger. She was itching to talk to her.

The day was a beautiful one.  The lake was shimmering with the reflection of the full, golden sun. The sky was clear and the air felt fresh, not too hot or cold.  It would've been a perfect day to take a boat out on Millerton Lake.  Instead, the place was cordoned off with crime scene tape and various officials doing their job to investigate a crime scene.

Miguel led Gina to the water's edge.  He wanted to see the victim before they started talking to witnesses. He'd learned early in his career that the crime scene itself told you a lot.  It often guided his investigations.  Gina knew it too, so she followed.

"I thought she was found face down?" Miguel asked the uniform as they stood in front of the body of Grace Collins.  Her blonde hair was fanned out all around her, the front of her clothes blood-stained.  Her throat was visibly slashed, it but looked more like Hollywood make-up after bleeding out and lying in water all night.

"She was.  Miss Ames, the jogger who found her, pulled her out of the water thinking maybe she was hurt or drowning.  She didn't realize she was dead until she fished her out."

Victoria Delatorre knelt beside the body, gloves on, her dark hair pulled back from her face in a tight bun. Miguel and Gina were happy to see her on the scene. She was an ME they really trusted and enjoyed working with.

"Time of death?" Gina asked Victoria.

"Judging by what I see, I'd say around midnight. But water can speed up the process, so I won't know for sure until we get her on the table."  Victoria stood to look the detectives in the eye.  She smiled at them.  "Glad to see you two are working the case."

Miguel nodded.  "Likewise."

"Unofficially, it looks like whoever did this to her beat her up pretty good first. She was dumped in the water as a last effort, like they were simply throwing out the trash," Victoria explained.    Her professional demeanor had returned.

"We'll want a rape kit done," Gina said.

"Of course," Victoria agreed.

"She looks young," Miguel commented.

"Seventeen, according to her driver's license," Victoria said, pointing at a purse that had already been bagged and tagged for evidence.

"Geez, what's this world coming to?"  Gina shook her head.  She saw murder victims often in this line of work, but it never got easier.  And a teenaged girl whose life ended so brutally was tough to stomach.  Who could possibly have wanted to hurt this pretty little thing?

A female deputy handed a piece of paper to Miguel.  "Here's Miss Ames' statement. She's ready to leave."

Miguel looked at Gina and then gestured toward the young lady who had found their vic.  He knew his partner well enough to know she wouldn't want a piece of paper in lieu of talking to the witness.  She was a good read on people and she needed them in person.

The trees cast a nice, long morning shadow around Miss Ames, standing as she was near the thicket. The hiking trail she had likely been running on was just a few feet away.

"Miss Ames?" Gina asked as she approached.

"Becca," the jogger corrected. She couldn't be more than mid-twenties, so Miguel assumed the formal salutation made her feel older than she was. Her hair was pulled back into a ponytail, her outfit sporty but also stylish. She certainly dressed like someone who came from a family of means. This wasn't just some T-shirt and sweats. But Becca gripped her own waist, as if she would crumble to the ground if she let go of herself. Her face was tear-stained and creased with worry lines.

"Becca," Gina smiled. Gina was great at putting people at ease. "I'm Detective Malone and this is Detective Alvarez. I know you gave a statement, but we just wanted to talk to you really quickly and then you can be on your way."

"Of course. I don't want whoever did this out on the streets. Where I jog..." Becca's voice trailed off and she began to chew on her fingernail. Likely she was picturing how easily it could've been her. Perhaps someone was lurking in the bushes waiting for a victim to come jogging by.

"About what time did you come across the body?" Gina asked, careful not to say the victim's name. They would need confirmation of the identity before publicly disclosing. And the press had a way of running with the slightest rumor.

Becca cleared her throat and swallowed hard. "I always start my run at 7:30 am, so it was probably around 7:45 that I saw something...ummm, her, floating in the water. At first I wasn't sure what it was. It looked kinda like clothing floating there. But when I saw it was a person, I instinctively pulled her out of the water thinking maybe she needed me to save her life. Do mouth to mouth or something."

"So you pulled her out and then what?" Miguel

added.

"Well, I saw the gash in her throat but also she just looked...wrong.  I don't know much about dead bodies, but I could tell something was wrong.  I called the Sheriff immediately."

"You did the right thing."  Gina placed a comforting hand on the young woman's arm.

"Did you notice anything suspicious?  See anyone nearby watching?  Anything like that?" Miguel asked.

Becca shook her head.  "No.  No one was around.  There weren't even boats out on the lake yet, which I guess is kinda surprising considering it's such a beautiful day."

"Was her purse with her when you found her?" Gina asked.

"Yes.  It was dangling around her neck like a necklace."

"Is there anything else you can think of that we should know?" Miguel asked.

"Well, I'm not positive," Becca said and then

sighed.  "But I think I've seen that girl out here before.  On my morning runs.  She looks familiar."

That piqued the detectives' interest.  Gina looked at Miguel with a raised eyebrow.  "What was the girl you saw doing out here those other times you might've seen her?"

Becca shrugged.  "Just hanging out.  There was a small handful of kids just laughing and talking out by the lake.  Didn't really strike me as anything but kids having fun.  Until today."

"How many kids would you say?" Miguel asked.

"Four or five," Becca said.

"Can you describe any of the other kids you saw?"

Becca shook her head.  "Not really.  A couple girls, a couple boys.  Nothing really to notice.  They just looked like average teenagers hanging out at the lake.  I didn't take any mental notes.  I didn't know I needed to until now."

"Thank you, Becca.  You've been really helpful.  If

you think of anything else, I want you to call me or Detective Malone directly."  Miguel handed her a card with their contact information on it.

"And if you want mental health professionals, ask about it, okay?" Gina said gently, gesturing toward the young female deputy who had handed them Becca's written statement.

As Miguel and Gina walked away from the frightened jogger, Gina asked Miguel, "So do you think the purse is really hers?"

"You don't?"

Gina squinted, looking up at her partner, the sun directly behind him brightening the clear morning sky.  "I don't know.  Something about it seems strange.  You beat this girl up, slash her throat, dump her in the water, but leave her purse with her?  It's like they didn't even try to hide anything."

Miguel shrugged.  "A crime of passion.  Teenage boy panics and just dumps and runs.  Impulse kills rarely cover their tracks well, you know that."

"Yeah, maybe.  I say we talk to her family. Confirm she is Grace Collins and then find out if she had a boyfriend, any enemies."

"Yeah, good idea.  But I can't stop thinking about that woman who called me this morning," Miguel said in a quieter tone to Gina.  Even talking about it made him feel crazy.

"Crazy lady on line two?"

Miguel nodded.  "She said Grace Collins. Identified our vic before we knew she was one.  And she said it like she knew something."

"So you thinking now maybe she really is psychic?"  Gina wrinkled her brow in confusion.

"Or she's an accessory or a witness.  Either way, she knows something."

Gina shrugged.  Their caseloads had only been getting larger the past few months.  And she and Miguel were a good team, and no good deed ever went unpunished on the force.  The more they solved, complete with convictions, the more they got the meatier cases.  There was no sense in fighting it.  They just had to do their jobs.  "Let's add the crazy lady to our interview list," she said.

# 4.

Daphne hung up from leaving yet another message for Detective Alvarez. She felt certain he was going to want to hear what she had to say.

"Don't worry, Grace." Daphne spoke to the ghost in her living room. "They always come around. Some just take longer than others."

The spirit of the girl before her looked a fright. Her hair was still tangled with driftwood and leaves, her clothes wet and disheveled, the gaping slash in her throat still raw and flapping. And her eyes were wide like saucers.

Daphne approached her. Of course, she knew there was no use in touching her, but she knew she needed to comfort her.  As a medium, Daphne and her moods were greatly affected by the emotional energy that the ghosts gave off.  The fear this girl was generating was giving Daphne a stomachache.

"He can't hurt you anymore, Grace.  You're already dead.  Please relax," Daphne explained.  "And think of a time in your life when you were happy.  What happy memory do you have?"

Grace tightened her mouth as she thought back through her brief life.  It had been a happy one.  She'd had a loving, supportive family and always lots of friends.  Her voice was soft like music when she said, "I remember when I got my puppy, Morty, for Christmas."

"There you go.  A puppy.  Morty was a beagle?" Daphne asked, confirming the images Grace was pushing into her mind.  She saw a young girl with braids getting her face licked repeatedly by a small puppy with floppy ears.

Grace softened as she remembered her sweet Morty.  "Yes."  Her trembling was slowing down and the fear she was emanating was reducing. Daphne felt better already.  The last thing she wanted was to be a basket case when she finally spoke to Detective Alvarez.  She needed him to trust her, like Detective Cayman in the LAPD had.  But she'd spent years working with Detective Cayman to get to that point.

When she wasn't working paranormal investigations of hauntings with Duncan and Duane, she had been helping the Los Angeles Police Department on cold homicide cases with Detective Cayman.

Detective Cayman was one of those good ole boys who looked the part of a cop, from head to toe.  He couldn't work undercover if his life depended on it.  And he was gruff, his manners as much as his appearance.  And yet, from day one, he'd never questioned Daphne or her methods.  "Every lead's a good lead until proven otherwise," he always used to say.

Daphne smiled at the memory and wondered if Detective Alvarez would be like Cayman.  She missed the work she did with the old lug.  It felt meaningful.  She couldn't bring the dead girls back to life, but she could help them find justice and deliver a bit of closure to the families. And somehow that felt like enough.

But Cayman had retired and Duane had broken her heart. And she was tired of the ghosts that swirled around her in Los Angeles. She was tired of the traffic and the fakeness of tinsel town. Even the name tinsel town made her want to punch something. She wanted a fresh start. A new backdrop where she could live in peace. And here she was—doing the same old thing she'd always done.

Daphne sighed. She'd never truly expected to outrun spirits.

So now to help Grace present herself a little nicer, even if Daphne was the only one who could see her. She didn't want to stare at Grace's slashed throat every day until the investigation was over.

"Now imagine yourself at school or hanging out with your friends. What kind of clothes did you wear? How did you style your hair?" Daphne asked.

Slowly, Grace's hair transformed from a tangled mess to smoothed, curled blonde locks, gently bouncing on her shoulder. She looked down at herself and then her clothes morphed into a tank top with a miniskirt and a flowery, flowing vest over the whole thing. She had cute ankle boots to complete the outfit and a low-hanging necklace.

Daphne shrugged. "Very stylish, Grace. You look more like yourself now."

Grace smiled at that. She had lived a beautiful life, which would now forever be defined by her traumatic death. The best she could do was stay by Daphne's side until the bastard was behind bars.

"He'll kill again," Grace told Daphne.

"Yeah, he seems like a real winner," Daphne snorted. Sure, she'd met with some dark spirits and angry souls in her time, but all in all she still felt that the dead were easier to deal with than the living. Ghosts were past judgement and the material things that didn't matter in the long run. They weren't always trying to manipulate you or backstab you or embarrass you.

She spared a glance at her phone, as if that would magically make it ring.

When she looked up, she saw Grace's intense eyes staring at her.  She was still afraid, but this time it wasn't from her own ordeal.  She was worried about his newest victim.

He had chosen a new girl.  And he would do it all again.

Daphne grabbed her phone and her purse, a small cross-body, and marched to the front door.  "Fine. He doesn't come to me, I'll go to him.  I need *you* to find out everything you can about his newest victim."

Grace, now looking like the ghost of a cute seventeen-year-old and no longer the murder victim she was, nodded with wild eyes. This softened Daphne a bit.

"We're going to get him, Grace.  I won't stop until we do."

Grace said nothing.  Daphne watched as she dematerialized right there in her living room.  With a dramatic slamming of her door, Daphne left her apartment and drove downtown.

# 5.

"Mrs. Collins?" Miguel flashed his badge at the woman standing in the doorway, and Gina did the same. He could tell by the puffy eyes and heavy look that she knew what this was all about. "I'm Detective Alvarez and this is Detective Malone with the Fresno Police Department. I trust you know why we're here?"

He didn't want to have to say the words out loud if he didn't have to.  It was always the worst part of the job.

Mrs. Collins nodded.  "You found my baby."

Miguel swallowed and then continued.  "We'd just like to ask you a few questions that might help us find out who did this to your daughter."

Mrs. Collins opened the door wide enough to let the detectives in and then turned and led them to a small sitting room to the right.  There was a large front window that Mrs. Collins had covered with small house plants.  The beautiful day continued and the natural light came pouring in, filling the room with warmth.  *Ironic that the room is warm and my heart is cold*, Mrs. Collins thought to herself.

"I already told the Sheriff's office that I know who did it," Mrs. Collins announced as she sat on the edge of her floral-patterned couch.

Miguel looked at Gina and raised an eyebrow just as they each took a seat across from Mrs. Collins.  "Oh?" Miguel fished a notebook and pen out of the front pocket of his blazer.

"Yes.  It was Rick."  Mrs. Collins twisted her hands in her lap, nervously rubbing them together as if the action could soothe her soul.  She was dry-eyed, but the weight of recent events was clearly having an impact on her psyche.  She looked like she'd just run a marathon carrying a sack of bricks.  Heavy lines accentuated what would otherwise be a beautiful face. She certainly didn't look more than early forties.  But grief had a way of adding years to your appearance in an instant.  Miguel knew that well from all the years as a homicide detective.

Gina jumped in.  "And who's Rick?"

"Grace's boyfriend."  Mrs. Collins rubbed her knees.  "I told her he was no good, driving around in that flashy sports car.  You know he never once even stepped foot in this house?  What kind of man dates a young girl and never even bothers introducing himself to her parents?"

"Does Rick have a last name?" Miguel asked.

Mrs. Collins pursed her lips together, creating large divots in her skin.  "Like I said, he never introduced himself.  I only know him as Rick."

"Was he a boy from Grace's school?" Gina asked.

Mrs. Collins shook her head.  "No, he was older. Maybe college age?"

Gina scooted a bit closer to the edge of the

loveseat she and Miguel were sitting on.  "Can you describe Rick?  Was he tall?  Short?  Any distinguishing features?"

Mrs. Collins snorted.  "Well. The best I could see from watching out this front window, he was tall, muscular.  His hair was brown and curly.  He looked like he could be a jock or something.  Always dressed in sweats and a T-shirt."

"You mentioned a sports car, Mrs. Collins," Miguel prodded.  "Can you describe it?"

Mrs. Collins fanned the air to wave away the notion that she had any details.  "I don't know anything about cars.  It was red.  And it looked expensive.  It was a convertible."

"Do you think any of Grace's friends might know more about Rick?" Gina asked, remembering how the jogger this morning had thought she'd seen Grace up at the lake with a group of friends.

"I would imagine Ellie would.  She's been Grace's best friend since elementary school.  Even if she never met him she would've at least heard—" Mrs. Collins swallowed before continuing. "—details. Here. I think I have her phone number in my contacts."

While Mrs. Collins scrolled through her phone for Ellie's information, Miguel asked her, "You said you know Rick did this. Is this just a mother's intuition? Or did you see something?"

"Oh, no." Mrs. Collins handed her phone to Gina so she could write down Ellie's name and number, and then she looked straight at Miguel. "Grace told me."

Miguel cocked his head to the side. "Grace told you this guy was going to kill her?"

Mrs. Collins shook her head. "No, last night. She came to me in my dream and told me he had done it. But not to worry because she was working with a psychic who would help solve the case." She took her phone back from Gina, and Gina tried to remain impassive, even as Miguel looked openly skeptical. "Have you talked to the psychic yet?" Mrs. Collins added.

"Not yet," Gina answered, staring at Miguel. It

was starting to be clear they couldn't avoid her forever.

"Mrs. Collins, is your husband home?" Miguel asked.

"No." Mrs. Collins cleared her throat and looked at the floor. "He's at the morgue identifying the body and making arrangements. I didn't need to see her that way." She looked up at Miguel. "Besides I know it's her."

"From the dream?" he asked.

She nodded. "It may seem strange to you, but I believe in the spiritual world." She toyed with the crucifix around her neck. "Sometimes the truth is right there before your eyes. And sometimes you can't see it. You have to feel it in your heart."

Miguel stood up. "I believe you. But I have to have evidence to lock the guy up."

"Thank you, Mrs. Collins." Gina stood as well.

Mrs. Collins remained sitting, her eyes beginning to brim with tears. "You're going to catch him, right?"

"We won't stop until we do," Miguel responded honestly. Regardless of where she got her information, boyfriends were certainly always a good place to start. He felt in his bones getting a last name from Ellie wasn't going to be the hardest thing in the world. This just might be a quick one, after all.

"If you think of anything else, or if your husband has anything to add, don't hesitate to call us," Gina said, handing Mrs. Collins her card, and she and Miguel let themselves out.

As they walked to the car, Gina asked with a half-smile on her face, "You think Grace's ghost visited her mom last night?"

Miguel shook his head at Gina, refusing to take the bait. "If she did, her ghost certainly gets around." He opened his car door and climbed in as Gina hopped in the passenger seat. "Let's get a last name on the boyfriend. There's no way he doesn't have something to tell us."

"You know, the testimony of a ghost has been used in court before," Gina told him.

"Are you punking me?"

Gina laughed and shook her head. "No, honest to

God.  The Greenbrier Ghost, as she's known.  Supposedly her ghost appeared to her mom and told her that her husband had murdered her.  That testimony convicted him."

"During the Salem Witch Trials or something?"

"No, around 1900.  I mean, it *was* a while ago but not *that* long ago," Gina said, still smirking.

"Hey, I'm not saying I won't take a little help where I can get it, but can you just get me a last name for Rick?  From someone who has a body, please."

Gina laughed again.  "I'm just sayin'."

Miguel noticed she had a smart-ass look the whole way back to the station.

# 6.

"Remember the crazy lady who called you this morning?" Officer Long whispered conspiratorially to Miguel, leaning way in to keep her voice low.

"Yeah, she's left me a dozen messages," Miguel responded. "I'm not entirely sure what to do with her."

"Well, I hate to be the one to tell you this, but she's here. And she's asking for you."

"Here?" Miguel looked over his shoulder at Gina, who shrugged in return. They were back in the middle of the bullpen, ready to get going on gathering intel.

"I like this psychic. She's persistent." Gina held her desk phone in her hand. "Go talk to her. You might as well. I'll follow up with Ellie and see what I can find out."

Miguel sighed heavily and pointed at Gina. "You owe me."

Gina shook her head. "Just do your job."

With heavy, slumped shoulders, Miguel headed to the front desk where visitors would wait. He was annoyed and he felt this lady was just a distraction from the work he needed to do. But as much as it bothered him, he knew Gina was right. After all the calls and showing up here, he might as well just hear her out. She wasn't going to make it easy to ignore her.

And she was on the interview list anyway. She seemed to at least know *something*, whatever her story was.

When he turned the corner, he saw a cute lady with blonde hair so light it almost looked white. It was short, but stylish, and somehow it suited her well. He realized in an instant that he'd expected an old crone in a muumuu with a large chunky necklace and her hair in a turban. A young, cute, stylish lady was far from what his imagination had cooked up.  Maybe this wasn't her?  But there was no one else there.

"Detective Alvarez, nice to meet you."  Daphne stuck out her hand.  It wasn't a question.  She knew it was him.  Miguel wondered if she was always this confident, or if it was just a façade she'd developed over the years. He shook her hand.  It was soft, he noticed.  Weirdly, he fought the urge to kiss it.

"Uh, Daphne, was it?" Miguel asked.  He figured "Crazy Lady" wouldn't go over so well.  And now that she was standing there in front of him, the moniker didn't even seem to suit.  He couldn't believe it, but he was mesmerized by her.

"Daphne Winters.  Yes.  I need to tell you what I know about Grace's murder."  Daphne cut straight to the chase.  She'd never been one for chitchat and baloney. Life was too short for all that.  And no one knew that better than she.

Miguel looked around.  He didn't really want to have this conversation right here in the open.  He'd never live it down the rest of his days on the force.  He gestured toward the hall.  "Let's talk in here."

Daphne followed him to a small room with a table and two folding chairs.  She assumed it was an interrogation room.  It was cold and sad.  Despite all her years working with the LAPD, she had never been forced into one of these rooms before.  She'd always been at a desk or on the phone.

Step one, this guy needed to trust her.  "Here."  She handed Miguel a piece of paper.

"What's this?"

"Detective Winslow Cayman, retired LAPD Cold Cases.  He and I worked together for years.  Call him.  He can provide references."  Daphne sat and leaned back in the chair.

He didn't look like he planned to call as he stuffed the paper in his pants pocket.

So Daphne tried another tactic.  There was some benefit to being able to read people.  "Your Tia Lencha.  She wanted you to be a lawyer. She still watches over you from time to time because she thinks you chose the dangerous path."

Miguel winced a bit at this. "You've done your homework." Before she'd passed, his Tia Lencha had been a formidable presence in his life. And she had been very disappointed when he joined the Academy after getting his criminal justice degree instead of going to law school. But he wanted to be where the action was, not pushing paper and playing politics.

Little did he know back then that there's paper pushing and politics in everything.

"I want you to trust me. Have faith in what I'm going to tell you. And I know you don't believe," Daphne stated flatly.

She didn't appear to be offended. He didn't want to believe, but something about this cute psychic was softening his resolve—and he wasn't about to admit it to himself or anyone.

"What do you know?"

"His name is Rick," Daphne started.

At this, Miguel leaned in.  She did know something.  He nodded as he spoke. "The boyfriend. We're looking into him.  Do you happen to know Rick's last name?"

Daphne snorted.  "Boyfriend? Who told you that? If Grace were here she'd likely say that was disgusting."

So the ghost could supposedly come and go?  He had questions about that, too, but he tabled them for now.  "So who is this guy, then?"

"He was her boss.  And a murderer, among his many talents," Daphne explained.

"Okay, back up.  The mom said he would pick her up in this fancy car.  What kind of boss does that?"

"Rick Bersin preys on teenage girls and 'hires' them to be in his films."  Daphne leaned in.  "They're porn movies.  And, in Grace's case, a snuff film.  He makes whatever films he gets hired to make.  Promises the girls stardom, blah blah, uses them and discards them."

Miguel chewed his lip and then pulled out his

notebook.  It didn't feel credible somehow, but he could at least look into it.  He wrote down *Bersin* as a name to research.

"It's not his real name, obviously," Daphne stated as if she could read his thoughts—or maybe she could. "But I guess it gets you started.  He calls his business Born Stars—I'm sure no coincidence it sounds like 'porn stars'—and his logo has a large star in the middle."

"You've seen his logo?"  Miguel raised an eyebrow even as he scribbled down the business name.

"Yeah, Grace showed me.  I see it like a photograph in my mind."

Suddenly the room felt very hot to Miguel.  He chastised himself for taking any of this seriously, for even entertaining this crazy lady as a witness.  How would he explain his lead to the D.A.'s office?  The ghost showed her a photo in her mind?  He stood up.  He had to end this before he got sucked into the delusion.  He could already feel himself starting to believe what she was telling him.

But Daphne was quick.  She reached out and grabbed his hand, firmly, with a tight grip.  This was much more forceful than their original handshake and her touch sent a shockwave straight to his soul.  His eyes widened in reaction.  It was as if she could reach inside of him, past the skin, past his flesh and blood.  And he wasn't scared.  A bit shocked, but somewhat at peace.  The whole sensation was surreal.  He stared at her in amazement and wonder as she spoke her next words.

"He has killed before and he'll do it again.  He can't have a bunch of teenagers running around able to identify him."  Daphne loosened her grip on Miguel's hand, but she didn't let go.  He was surprised to find he didn't want her to.  "I called you a bunch of times and finally came here because he's chosen his next victim.  And Grace told me who it was."

Miguel was a great detective.  His record was impeccable.  He followed the rules, the law and the facts.  If he had had even an inkling of the desire his Tia Lencha had felt for him to become a lawyer, he always knew he'd have been a great one.  But suddenly, here and now with this pretty little psychic, he didn't know which end was up.  Was this a dream?  Was it real?  Did she actually know something? Or was she truly delusional?

He shook his head, trying to process what she was telling him.  Grace wasn't some one-off.  There was a big operation going on and she was one of many pawns on the chessboard.  Could he afford not to take it seriously?  Was there any harm in looking into the *Born Stars* business?

Miguel stuck his chin out as he questioned Daphne.  "What's her name?"

"Ellie."

Miguel felt the blood drain from his face.  The best friend.  The girl her mom thought might know something about this Rick guy.

Daphne finished the thought.  "Ellie Markham. Grace's best friend."

Without further analyzing the truths Daphne might or might not be speaking, without stopping to again question her unconventional methods, Miguel ran from the interrogation room as fast as he could, leaving Daphne alone.

Daphne stood up and announced, "Well.  I guess my work is done here.  I'll just see myself out."

# 7.

Miguel raced back to Gina's desk, overwhelmed with the concern that it would be too late.  He leaned over her desk, panting as he did so.  "Please tell me you got a hold of Ellie."

Gina straightened up the papers on her desk and stared at Miguel.  He looked like a man who hadn't properly used his vacation time.  "She didn't answer.  So I found her mom's contact information."

"And?"

"Geez, Miguel.  We'll get a last name.  Does everything have to be the instant it pops in your head?"  Gina leaned way back in her seat.  She trusted Miguel and was really thankful he was her partner, but at this moment she wanted to kick him.

"She could be in trouble.  We might need to do an APB.  What did her mom say?"  Miguel swung around and sat on Gina's desk, his arms folded across his chest.

Gina waited for more information but it didn't come.  "And you know this because?"

Miguel looked up at the ceiling.  Gina already knew who he'd been talking to.  There wasn't much he could do to avoid telling her the truth, even as he cringed at the sound of it coming from his mouth.  "Daphne, the psychic.  She told me some interesting things.  Including that Grace wasn't his first and won't be his last.  His next victim is Ellie."  He found himself talking fast, trying to convince Gina.  Maybe if Gina said she believed, he wouldn't feel so vulnerable having fallen for it.

But Gina didn't really react one way or the other.  She chewed her lip and then picked up her desk phone.  "I haven't called her mother yet."

Miguel nodded before standing up and walking over to his own desk across from Gina's.  He willed himself to remain calm, even though inside his stomach was in knots with the worry that it might be too late for Ellie.  He watched Gina dial and he pretended to do something at his desk, shuffling papers uselessly as if he were being constructive.  He wanted to look up the company *Born Stars* but he couldn't make his fingers type.  He was too curious if there was even anything to worry about.  Had a psychic just taken him down a rabbit hole?  All of a sudden he had a sinking feeling that he had jumped the gun.  Why did he panic based on the random testimony of a crazy lady?  Man, he was really losing it.

As he heard Gina wrap up the call with Ellie's mother, he started to apologize, but Gina cut him off. "They haven't seen or heard from Ellie in days."

The roller coaster he was on bounced him between skepticism and devout faith, and he was spinning from it all. "What?"

"They're not worried yet because she sometimes stays with friends for a few days at a time. I get the sense she's a bit of a free spirit.  But given that her best friend turned up dead, well, that changes things."  Gina folded her hands across her desk.  "Are we believing the psychic now?"

"I don't think we should completely rule out her information without at least looking into it," Miguel stated, trying to remain levelheaded even as he felt like he was spiraling fast.  In the furthest corners of his mind, a place he definitely did not want Gina probing, he had to admit that he *did* believe Daphne.  Or, more importantly, whether he believed was immaterial.  He was petrified that her prediction was right.  And they were too late.  In life-or-death situations, he couldn't afford not to take information like this seriously. The stakes were way too high.  "She told me Rick's last name was Bersin.  And that that was likely a pseudonym.  She also said he used these girls to make X-rated films for high-paying clientele, and then to save his own skin he 'disposed of' the girls when he was done.  His film company is called *Born Stars*."

"That sounds like a shady company.  Who would fall for it?"

"Teenaged girls looking for stardom, I guess."

"So, according to this psychic, there have been other girls used and discarded?" Miguel nodded in response to Gina's question. "So there should be other girls out there either missing or dead tied to this case?"

"Let's pull the list of all girls aged fourteen to twenty who either died mysteriously or were never found."

"All right. I'll tackle that. What are you going to do?"

"I'm going to see what I can find out about Rick Bersin and the Born Stars. We gotta find this guy if we're going to find Ellie before something bad happens."

"Looks like it might be time for that All Points Bulletin."

Miguel rubbed his chin. He didn't want to panic, but he also didn't want to talk to another grieving mother this week. "What about an Amber Alert also?"

"We don't know she was kidnapped, Miguel. Hell, we don't even know that she's anything. Let's just treat her as missing until we can find out the truth."  Gina leaned on her desk to talk to Miguel.  She was worried too.  It certainly wasn't comforting that the best friend of their murder victim hadn't been home in days.  But she didn't want to panic, and she knew Miguel well enough to know he didn't want to either.

"You're right.  We gotta focus on this Rick guy. He's our true lead."  Miguel started typing the name into his database.

Gina shook her head as she herself got to work on the APB and pulling the report of missing girls.  "He probably has a skinny, creepy mustache, too.  Can't he just find women who *want* to be porn stars?  Why does he have to lure teenagers and then kill them?"

Miguel leaned back in his chair.  "Let's add that to the list of things we ask the bastard when we find him. Daphne said Grace's film was a snuff film, so I don't think he's making your run-of-the-mill porn movies."

Gina looked visibly shocked.  "As in, Grace was *murdered* on film?"

Miguel shrugged. "Supposedly."

Gina tapped her finger on the desk. "We don't have to just find Rick. We gotta get that film. This is huge."

Miguel smiled. "So you're starting to believe Daphne, too, huh?"

Gina smiled even bigger. "So she's Daphne now, huh?"

Miguel went back to his computer and ignored Gina. Also, he wasn't completely sure that he wasn't blushing. And why? Daphne *was* pretty but that didn't mean anything. He saw pretty girls every day. But then he remembered when she'd touched him. The sensation was more than just a pretty girl touching him. It was more like she'd lit his soul on fire.

But that was ridiculous.

"Holy shit," Miguel announced. He continued explaining to Gina before she could even ask what he was talking about. "This guy is all over the internet. He's not even trying to be black market."

Gina came around to look over Miguel's shoulder. "Or he's the world's dumbest criminal."

"He *is* a filmmaker. A legitimate one if this can be believed. He makes corporate and brand films for businesses throughout the Central Valley." He scrolled down and an inset of a handsome, clean-cut man with perfectly gelled hair came on screen. "Look at that. No mustache."

"This could be like a dating profile and he used a pic from fifteen years ago. Now he's fat and bald with a skinny mustache."

"There's no address but there is a phone number." Miguel scribbled it down on his notepad.

"Just talk to tech. Spencer can get you an address associated with that website in his sleep," Gina said before walking back to her desk. "Then we don't tip him off. We just show up and ask him about Grace. See what he says. Whether or not he killed her is one thing, but we do have at least one witness that says they were hanging around with one another."

Agreeing with her logic, Miguel walked down the hallway to Tech.  Spencer was one of Miguel's and Gina's favorites because he was so good at his job.  Evidence that was encrypted?  No problem.  Someone tried to wipe their hard drive?  This kid didn't bat an eye.  He was sitting at his desk, typing something into his PC that to Miguel looked like gobbledygook.

"What ya working on?" Miguel asked as he pulled up a chair next to Spencer.

Spencer pulled his long hair out of his way and slid the Mountain Dew he'd been drinking down the desk.  His clothes were baggy and wrinkled, like he hadn't changed or slept in days.  And maybe he hadn't.

"This is for the drug bust on the South Side from last week.  Seems one of the guys was dumb enough to keep his contacts on a PC in his closet.  Basic encryption.  He didn't even swing for something high-tech." Spencer shook his head.  Sure, there were really smart cyber criminals out there that gave Spencer the occasional challenge, but mostly Miguel assumed Spencer went around thinking the average criminal was a complete moron.  Not everyone they arrested in Southeast Fresno was a computer whiz.

"I need a quick and easy favor.  I need an address associated with a website," Miguel explained.

"Easy?  That's baby stuff," Spencer snorted.  Miguel handed him the website address and waited for him to do his magic.  Spencer typed frantically and not even a minute later he had something.

"It's registered to Kevin Kyle.  Ooh, he lives in Clovis.  Fancy."  Spencer printed the address and handed it to Miguel.

Miguel frowned.  "Hmmmm...we're looking for a Rick Bersin.  We thought this was his website."

Spencer typed frantically into his computer keyboard before shaking his head.  "Nope.  Rick Bersin looks like a baloney name."  He tapped the paper Miguel was holding.  "This guy is real.  Registered with the DMV."

"Kevin Kyle.  All right."  Miguel stood up and started walking before he turned around.  "Thanks for the baby stuff, Spencer!"

"Bring me a challenge next time, Mikey!" Spencer said without turning around.

Miguel's thoughts were all over the place as he walked back to his desk.  Could Kevin Kyle be Rick Bersin?  Or an accomplice?  Was this more evidence that Daphne was right?  He fought the sudden urge to call her with this information to get her take on it.

Regardless they were going to have to pay a visit to this Kevin of Clovis.

But before he went on a drive again with Gina, there was something he wanted to do.

# 8.

"This is Cayman," the former cold case detective of the Los Angeles Police Department answered the phone with a no-bullshit attitude. Miguel liked him already.

"Detective Winston Cayman? Retired LAPD?"

"The one and only. What can I do for you?" Cayman's voice was cordial, but the tone had a skeptical tilt to it, as if Miguel's answer was a very important one in his deciding how quickly to hang up.

"I'm calling about Daphne Winters." Miguel decided to get to the point before Cayman gave up on the call entirely. Who knew how hounded this man was by reporters and such? "I'm Detective Miguel Alvarez and I'm working with Ms. Winters on a homicide case here in Fresno County."

"Ahh, Daphne." His tone instantly changed from guarded to friendly. His admiration for the psychic was evidenced in the smile that came through his voice. "You're lucky, then. She's the best."

"So." Miguel struggled with exactly how to phrase his question. He'd wanted someone to vouch for her, but he hadn't exactly thought through how to ask that. "Her record with you was good?"

"More than good," Cayman huffed into the phone. "Flawless. In all the years we worked together, there was only one case we didn't close. And it was my fault, not hers. Although I know it weighs heavy on her heart."

"So I should trust her information?"

"Detective Alvarez," Cayman said, his voice still cordial but definitely at the same time scolding, "I don't know what her secret is, but whatever it is, it works. If she's on your case, consider it solved."

Miguel swallowed.  "That's good to hear."  It was what he'd hoped, and even expected, to hear, but still, it was comforting.

"You know how I became the cold case detective with the best record in Los Angeles?  Two things.  I followed up on every lead, no matter how trivial.  And I trusted Daphne Winters.  A lead is a lead, no matter where it comes from.  Remember that," Cayman instructed.

Miguel nodded, even though Cayman couldn't see.  He liked this guy.  And Miguel already lived by the motto that a lead was a lead.  It was how his own record had gotten so good.  Sometimes the case load got so heavy that it was tempting to close a case quickly and follow the easiest crumbs, but it wasn't always the right way to be good at this job.  "I believe you.  And I trust her too.  She suggested I call you to vouch for her, so I followed up."

Cayman laughed a hearty laugh.  Miguel imagined a big man, weathered by a life of chasing the cases no one wanted.  And solving them.  Cayman said into the phone, "She's a ball buster, that one.  But honest to God, the best partner I ever had in my life."

"Thank you, Detective Cayman.  You've been incredibly helpful," Miguel said, as he looked up to see Gina watching him questioningly.  They said their good-byes and Miguel felt the need to explain to his partner. "LAPD.  He fully vouched for Daphne."

Gina shrugged and grabbed her keys.  "So far she hasn't given us a reason not to trust her.  I'm driving."

"Who's going through the missing persons list?" Miguel followed her through the bullpen toward the front glass double doors.

Gina rolled her eyes, even though Miguel was looking at the back of her head.  "I put Cunningham on it. How many cases are we going to work before you trust me?"

"I just wondered," Miguel said defensively, even though secretly he did have to swallow the urge to control every aspect of his investigations.  He knew Gina wouldn't drop any balls.  But somehow that knowledge didn't stop him from confirming.

"Sure you did.  Now let's go find out if Rick is actually Kevin.  And most importantly of all, if he has a mustache."  Gina wiggled her eyebrows and led the way to their Crown Vic.  Miguel begrudgingly climbed into the passenger's seat.  He liked to be the one to drive.

They talked a bit about the case on their way to Clovis, one city over, but inevitably the topic of Daphne popped up.

"Do you think she's actually psychic?  Like, is she actually getting her information from the ghost of the girl we fished out of Millerton Lake?" Miguel asked Gina, who kept her eyes on the road as she responded.

Gina shrugged.  "Why not? If someone has unfinished business here on earth before they enter the afterlife, I should think a murdered young girl has a cause."

"But...ghosts?"  Miguel shook his head.  "I'm not sure I believe in them."

"I never really thought about it one way or another either, but I suppose it's not *that* hard to believe."

"You don't think so?  To me it just seems so crazy.  Like we might as well solve our case with Tarot cards."

Gina huffed a laugh.  "You like to talk a big game, but if a lead came in the form of a Tarot Card and a Crystal Ball, you'd be following it.  Don't even try to tell me otherwise."  Miguel tried to fight a smile at Gina's teasing but couldn't.  He didn't argue either.  He *was* following up on the leads he was meanwhile calling crazy.  Gina continued, "You met her.  Did she seem crazy?"

Miguel thought about this for a moment before answering, even though he knew the answer right away.  He wanted to answer honestly, but cautiously, his desire to not be gullible driving his reactions.  When he pictured her in his mind, he saw a pretty face, a strong woman.  Maybe even a bit stubborn.  Rough around the edges but caring enough to listen to the souls of the departed.  And then the time she'd touched him...he couldn't deny she'd sent a tremor straight through to his soul.

"No," Miguel answered honestly. "Not at all, actually. The things she says *sound* crazy when you think about them, but when she was talking she came across as very credible."

"And the LAPD trusted her?"

"Yeah." Miguel leaned his head on his hand, his elbow rested up against the car door. "Spoke very highly of her, actually."

"Remember that case last year at the Live Oak apartments? How nothing quite fit together? We had all those clues, tons of evidence, but it all seemed to conflict with itself."

"I remember."

"But when we finally stopped overthinking it, we could see the truth. It *did* all fit together to tell a story. Just not the one we thought."

"Right. It wasn't a drug deal at all. It turned out to just be domestic violence gone wrong."

"Exactly." Gina pointed at Miguel.

"So what's your point?"

"My point is—" She parked the Crown Vic in front of Kevin Kyle's address. "—don't overthink everything. You miss stuff when you do. You're a good cop. You just need to learn to trust your instincts a little bit."

She cut the engine and they climbed out. The home they stood in front of was not the usual place they were called to. They were accustomed to talking to drug dealers, rough neighborhoods, gangsters. This place was a mansion, essentially. It had thick, stone columns on the front which held up a large white balcony on the second floor. There was even a fountain out front—a freaking fountain. Who was this Kevin Kyle guy?

Miguel looked over at Gina and she gave him the same look of incredulity that he was giving her. They'd been partners long enough that words weren't always needed. They walked past the immaculately groomed garden, roses and hedges that were precisely shaped exactly the same all across the front. Miguel got the sense if he pulled out a ruler, every bush would be identical in shape and dimension.

The front door was large and imposing.  It was bright red, and a double door, but more than that, it was very tall and much wider than average.  For sure, this was also custom dimensions.  A heavy bronze knocker hung on the door begging to be used.  Miguel obliged.  The knocker was as heavy as it looked and the force of its knocking could be felt as much as heard.

They waited in silence but not for very long.  A few moments later they heard feet scuffling on the other side of the door.  And then the sounds of latches and locks being undone before the large door handle turned and a man stood in front of them. He was wearing shorts and a bathrobe, a martini glass in one hand.

And no mustache.  He was clean-shaven and well-groomed.

"What can I do for you?" the man asked nicely enough, but the disappointment was evidenced all over his face.  Clearly he was expecting more enticing company than Gina and Miguel.

Miguel nodded at Gina to answer.  He knew this kind of man.  He would see Miguel as a threat, maybe even beneath him since Miguel was Mexican.  But a pretty woman would disarm him and maybe he'd be a bit more forthcoming.

"Mr. Kevin Kyle?" Gina asked.

The shirtless man jutted out his chin.  "Who's asking?"

Miguel took his cue from Gina and they flashed their badges.  "Detectives Alvarez and Malone. Fresno P.D. homicide division."

The man's eyes widened a bit, and Gina incorrectly assumed it was at the word homicide, but the man asked, "Fresno Police? What are you doing out here?"

Again Gina shared a look with Miguel which he understood correctly.  Homicide detectives show up at your door and you don't flinch, but the fact that they represent Fresno instead of Clovis is what pushes your buttons?

"We'd like to ask you a few questions about the Born Stars business and website."  Miguel thought it best to get as far as they could with this guy before they got a door in their face just for being from the "wrong city."

"That's not me."  And he folded his arms across his chest, very delicately balancing his fancy drink so it didn't slosh all over his bathrobe.

"Are you Kevin Kyle?" Gina asked again.

"Yeah, but I just helped make the website.  I don't have anything to do with the business," Kevin Kyle hurriedly explained.

"So you got this big, fancy house just from setting up the website?" Miguel asked, gesturing to the front of the mansion.

"Yeah. That's what I do," Kevin explained.  Miguel still watched him covering his body, guarded in every sense of the word.

"Make websites?" Gina clarified.

"Consulting," Kevin answered, again with his chin

jutting out defiantly.

"So you do consulting for Born Stars?" Miguel asked.

"No, I told you." Kevin looked at Miguel, and Miguel took note that his eyes held the tiniest sliver of fear. "All I did for them was make the website."

"So, in the course of this consulting, did you meet with Mr. Rick Bersin?" Gina shrewdly moved to the next topic.

"Uh, it was all mostly done over the phone." His eyes darted back and forth between the detectives.

"Mostly? So you did meet him at least once?" Gina asked. "And is that truly a photo of him on the website?"

"Well, it's the photo he gave me. I don't know the guy, I swear. Look, I'm expecting guests. How much longer is this going to be?"

"Just one more thing, Mr. Kyle." Miguel casually rested his hands on his hips, careful to pull back his jacket enough to allow the handgun in his holster to be evident.

"Do you happen to have a business card handy? For your consulting company?"

"Oh, yeah."   His shoulders relaxed, clearly relieved.  He disappeared into the house for a bit, but he reappeared and handed the business card to Miguel with confidence.  "Is that all?"

"Thank you, Mr. Kyle."  Gina nodded as Miguel stuffed Kyle's card in his jacket pocket.  They turned on the elaborate front porch and saw two young girls in bikini tops and cutoff jeans coming up the walkway, just passing the fountain.  Kevin Kyle's guests.

"He's too old for you," Miguel muttered as they passed on the walkway.  The girls did nothing but giggle, and the detectives climbed back into their car before continuing their conversation.

"He's lying," Miguel stated as Gina started the engine.

"Oh, he's so full of shit I almost flushed his martini."  Gina rolled her eyes.  "What's the business card say?"

Miguel pulled it out as Gina pulled away from the fancy Clovis home.  He angled it toward the bright light coming in the window and read, "KKK Consulting." Miguel let his hand fall to his lap, the card still gripped between his thumb and forefinger.  "Is he kidding with that shit?"

"So is he a white supremacist? Or is his name truly Kevin K. Kyle?"

"Who the fuck knows?  But I'm pretty sure he does more than make websites for the Born Stars." Miguel shoved the card back in his pocket, planning to do more research when they were back at HQ.

"He could be bankrolling the whole operation," Gina proffered.

"Or one of the high paying clients," Miguel theorized.

"Should we be worried about those girls we passed?" Gina asked, eyes still on the road as she drove.

"If he's that stupid then this case will be an easy one," Miguel responded, and slouched down in the passenger seat.  Something told him they weren't that lucky. And that they were a long way off from the end of the path this case was leading them down.

# 9.

"She's in the mountains," Daphne explained to Detective Cayman.  "This way."  She gestured behind herself and led the way, a team of police following her into the hills.  She climbed, shoving trees and brush out of her way as she did.  There was no footpath to follow.  She was following her internal compass, the one that only she could sense.  The one that the spirit of the victim was using to guide her.  "Over here."

And when she turned back to lead Detective Cayman, she noticed it was Detective Miguel Alvarez. She felt the overwhelming need to explain. "We have to find her. We can't leave her."

Miguel said nothing, so she kept climbing, leading

the team.  And until she reached the top, she kept climbing even though her legs felt heavy and tired. This was where she was.  A little girl sat on top of a large boulder, her floral-patterned dress splattered with blood. She had two ponytails, the one on the right sat much higher than the one on the left.  As Daphne neared, she noticed the ligature marks.

Someone had tortured her before they'd killed her.

"Why didn't you bring the good guys, Daphne?" the little girl asked with her singsong little voice.  And her words bothered Daphne.  Daphne turned around to show the little girl that the police were here, but there was no one.  Daphne stood alone on the mountain with the little girl.

"I did bring them, Maddy.  I did," Daphne shouted, anger and frustration causing her throat to tighten.  Why had they not followed her up the mountain?

"You have to find me, Daphne.  No one can but

you."

Daphne fell to her knees, crying. "I can't. You've got to give me more time."

"Find me, Daphne."

Maddy's voice was still echoing in Daphne's ears when she woke up, drenched in sweat. A tickle on her cheek told her that there were fresh tears running down her face. Daphne tore back her covers and stumbled to the kitchen. She'd had bothersome dreams her whole life. Even in sleep, she couldn't shake the dead.

But this was different.

Daphne poured herself two fingers of bourbon and watched the amber liquid swirl in her glass. Madison "Maddy" Laurens had been missing for twenty years when her case hit Detective Winston Cayman's desk. They had the crime scene—an abandoned house at the end of the Laurens family property. It was covered in Maddy's blood, her hair samples found on the scene, her bike found out front. Maddy had never made it home from school one fateful day and only her bike and blood were ever found. And there was no DNA evidence for the perpetrator.

So Cayman called Daphne.

Daphne knew that Maddy had been kept alive for days before she was murdered. She'd been tortured and molested at this evil man's hands. Maddy had shown Daphne his face and the police had a sketch artist draw him. But that's all they had. That and the fact that Maddy was buried somewhere in the mountains. But there were mountains all around Los Angeles, and Daphne could never get more out of Maddy's spirit.

The police sketch was as far as they ever got, and Cayman moved onto another case. The guilt ate at Daphne's soul and at first she'd dreamt about Maddy at least once a week. The dreams had gotten better since she'd left Los Angeles, but they still came every now and again.

That case still haunted her in every sense of the word.

And what was the meaning of Detective Alvarez

making an appearance?  He'd had nothing to do with Maddy's case, had he?

In one huge gulp, Daphne swallowed the bourbon.  It burned as it coated her throat and Daphne loved it, felt the heat as it landed in her belly.  She hated that she had to resort to this, but it was the only thing that gave her a moment's peace.  She loved Cayman as a father figure, but she hated him for giving up on Maddy.  So when things also fell apart in her relationship with Duane, she ran.  Ran like a little punk from her problems.

Daphne mentally chastised herself for being so weak.  She'd spent so much of her life pretending not to give a shit that it hurt doubly hard when she actually did.  She'd always known things would never work out with Duane.  Really, she just found him attractive with his muscled arms and brilliantly blue eyes.

The complete opposite of Miguel.

Miguel.  When did he stop being Detective Alvarez? And why did he keep popping up in her brain?

Groaning to herself, she padded back to her

bedroom, staring at the walls.  She wasn't scared of the dark or the nighttime.  She never had been.  She knew what lurked in the dark and, unlike the case for most people, it comforted her.  It comforted her to know that someone was always there, dead or alive.

It was her own thoughts and feelings that haunted her, not ghosts and things that go bump in the night.  Guilt over Maddy.  Guilt over Duane.  And what was it about Miguel?

She had known there was something the second she laid eyes on him.  There was a glow about him she'd never seen on anyone alive before.  And when she'd touched him, she'd felt a solid connection.  And she knew he felt it too.  She wasn't sure how to explain it, but it was like their souls recognized each other.  She'd never had that before with any human being.

She didn't know what to make of it, and that bothered her.

Miguel was handsome enough.  Maybe not hot like Duane, but he had that tall, dark and powerful thing going on.  But it wasn't even that.  She wasn't just physically attracted to him.  She was *connected* to him on some metaphysical level.  And that scared the living shit out of her.  More than ghosts.  More than dead bodies.  More than haunting dreams.

She was scared that her soul needed and wanted this man after she'd spent a whole lifetime making sure she didn't need anybody.

She slowly fell back to sleep trying to tell herself that those feelings weren't real, that they were just her imagination.  She dreamt of Miguel smiling at her.  She was chasing him, but they were laughing.  She would reach out to tag him, but always miss, him moving at just the last second.  It was playful and harmless.

"Daphne!"  Someone called to her from a distance.  It was a voice she'd never heard before.  A young woman's voice.  Daphne froze to listen, so Miguel stopped too.  He watched her, walking toward her as she listened to the woman calling her.  "Daphne.  I'm over here."

Daphne walked toward the voice.  It was off in the shadows.  Miguel was here standing in the light, so calming and comforting.  He reached out to her as if to beg her to stay with him. But she knew she had to go. This person needed her.  She had to face the shadows.

She turned to the darkness and stepped into the void. There was nothing but blackness, not a sliver of light crept through.  She followed the voice calling her—it was the only thing she had to tell her which way to go.  Slowly she walked, following the voice.

Up ahead appeared a small crack of light. Daphne raced toward it.  A door was slightly cracked. Just enough light peeked through that she could see the number 33 on a teal-colored door.  She pushed the door open wider and the voice calling her got louder.  A lone light bulb was on, casting a yellowish glow in a dirty motel room, complete with a hideous duvet on the double bed.

In the middle of the room, a teenage girl sat blindfolded, hands bound.  She had thick, brown, curly hair and she was dressed in a stylish outfit.

"Are you the one calling me?" Daphne asked the blindfolded girl.

"Daphne. Please, help me. It's not too late." The girl lifted her arms to show her bindings and Daphne caught a glimpse of the necklace she wore with a golden E dangling from it.

Again Daphne woke up, heart pounding.

This time, someone was with her in her room. A blonde ghost that had once looked a fright but now just looked like a sweet teenager: Grace.

Daphne swallowed hard and asked the ghost, "Is it Ellie? Does he have her?"

Grace nodded slowly and said, "Yes. We're running out of time. He'll film her tomorrow."

Heart jackhammering in her chest, Daphne looked at the clock. It was 5:25am. Cops worked weird hours, though, right? She didn't know what else to do. She grabbed her phone and called the man her soul trusted more than anyone else in the world: Detective Miguel Alvarez, Fresno P.D.

# 10.

"Gina, wake up," Miguel shouted into his phone as he hurriedly threw on his beige blazer and hunted all around his room for his shoes.

"What's going on?"  Gina's voice was groggy. She'd been deep in sleep.  And early morning was not her best hour of the day.

"Daphne knows where Ellie is.  Where Rick is keeping her," Miguel explained.  His shoes were right by his dresser and had been this whole time.  He shook his head at the irony.  "Meet us at the Palm Sway Motel on Blackstone."

"Us?"  Gina was more alert now, although her body was still struggling to get out of bed.

"Me and Daphne.  And supposedly Grace, if you're willing to believe that one," Miguel somewhat muttered.  He didn't want to admit it to himself, let alone Gina, but he actually was starting to believe.

"Wait for me, I'm right behind you.  And, Miguel." Gina sat up in bed.  "Get a warrant.  We can't put this guy away if we barge in his hotel without probable cause."

"See you in ten."  Miguel hung up the phone and stuffed it in his pocket.  His gun went in the holster next.  His badge last.  A quick peek out the window let him know it was going to be another gorgeous day.  *Why do the ugliest things always seem to happen on the most beautiful days?*

He drove quickly, but safely.  He had no way of knowing if the Born Stars preferred to make their snuff films in the morning or evening.  He just knew that time was of the essence.  And a young girl was trapped.  He hit his steering wheel with the palm of his hand, taking his frustration out on his car.  He wanted to punch Rick Bersin—and honestly Kevin K. Kyle of KKK Consulting too.

What kind of men were they?  Sadly, Miguel knew all too well what kind of men they were.  Black hearts and dark souls.

Miguel ran a hand through his thick, black hair.  Normally, it would be gelled in a clean-cut style.  Miguel had always been strait-laced when it came to his looks.  In fact, his family had made fun of him for it when he was younger.  Even when he was a kid, his hair was always short and styled, his clothes without wrinkle.  Tia Lencha had mentioned on more than one occasion that he was an old soul.  But today?  His shirt was one he'd grabbed from where it lay draped over a chair.  His hair was loose and without a drop of product.  At least it was cut short.  And Daphne wouldn't care, he knew that.  What he didn't know was why he cared if Daphne cared.

He hit his steering wheel again and slammed harder on the gas pedal.  He was just a few stoplights away from one of the larger streets in Fresno.  As a beat cop in his early days, he'd hang out near Blackstone to catch the drag racers, so he knew this area well.  Just up ahead, the sign for the Palm Sway flickered in the early morning light.  It was neon green and looked dated and worn.  He was impressed it still lit up, to be honest.  He followed it when the stoplight turned green, heading toward the seedy motel with the ugly light.  Fitting.  An ugly sign for an ugly man doing ugly deeds.  The urge to catch this murderer-slash-rapist-slash-filmmaker was overwhelming.  His knuckles were white when he finally turned into the Palm Sway parking lot and parked in front of a pink building with teal-colored doors.

Daphne was already waiting there standing next to what he assumed was her car.  Despite his emotions about Rick Bersin and Ellie, he smiled when he saw her.  Strange that her presence calmed him.

But she didn't smile back.

Her face was hard edges and worry lines.  She spoke before he'd even completely gotten out of his car.

"She's gone," Daphne blurted.  "He already moved her."

Miguel grabbed Daphne's shoulders as he

processed her words.  They were already too late?  He looked around at the ugly pink building, as if he could look through the walls and confirm Daphne's story.  He couldn't. Exactly.

"Which room did you say?  33?" Miguel asked, scanning the teal doors of the two-story motel.  Every color on this motel was brighter than the next.  Maybe they were trying to evoke a Florida vacation, but it looked more like it evoked two stars.

Daphne shook her head.  "Doesn't matter.  She's not there anymore.  We're too late."

Miguel gently cupped her chin, moved by the need to comfort the pretty psychic.  "There could still be evidence in there if they haven't cleaned it yet.  I'll have the front office open the room for me and we'll have a look, okay?"

Daphne thought about it for a second, looking deep into Miguel's eyes.  And then she nodded.  "Grace says she's still alive."

"Then we still have time.  We'll find her."

The sound of tires screeching as a car turned into the Palm Sway parking lot alerted them both to the fact that Gina had just arrived.  She parked and Daphne and Miguel walked over to her, meeting her as she emerged from her car.

"I was just about to head to the front office," Miguel said by way of greeting.  They were in synch enough that they didn't need pleasantries.  Gina looked like she'd had better mornings.  Her make-up was impeccable and her clothes were clean and pressed, but her eyes were sunken and puffy and she moved slowly.  And she didn't respond to her partner.

Gina looked right past Miguel to the blonde in the long dress and thick, black boots.  "You must be Miss Winters."

"Daphne," Daphne corrected.  Miguel noticed she didn't reach her hand out.  "Good morning, Detective Malone."

With a curt nod from Gina, Miguel turned to lead the way to the front office of the Palm Sway Motel.  If the exterior of the rundown motel looked cheap and haggard, the office was all that and more.  A light bell dinged as Miguel pushed on the glass front door, entering a room with teal-colored carpeting.  The light pink paint on the walls was dirty and chipped.  Water stains hung like paintings, adorning the walls with their blotches and splatters.  Perhaps Miguel imagined it, but the carpet felt sticky beneath his feet.

His clean-freak ways were set instantly on edge.

A small man in a white tank top sat with his feet up on the green front desk. *They need to hire themselves an interior decorator pronto.*  He looked up from the magazine he was perusing for only a brief second. "Whaddaya want?"

Miguel and Gina pulled out their badges.  "We need to see inside room 33.  We have a warrant."  He didn't really yet, but he hoped it was coming through any minute.

Still keeping his eyes cast away from the detectives and the psychic, he responded, "What's so special about that room?"

"Just open it. Now." Gina spoke curtly. She hadn't had her morning coffee yet, it was early, and she really wasn't in the mood for games.

He finally looked up and closed his magazine. He stared at Gina for a minute but still made no move to be helpful. Miguel was just about to start throwing around terms like "obstruction of justice" when Daphne took matters into her own hands.

"You can open room 33 or I can let them know what you sell out of room 2. It's your choice."

That got his attention. Still without speaking, he pulled his legs off the green front counter and stood up straight, eyes wide like he'd been caught with a dirty secret.

"Should I also get a warrant for room 2, or are we finally heading to room 33?" Miguel asked.

Wordlessly, the man grabbed a set of keys from the wall behind where he'd been sitting and walked out a side door. The detectives and Daphne followed.

Miguel leaned into Daphne and whispered, "Nicely done."

Daphne curled her lips into a tiny smirk, happy with the praise. He smelled rugged, like a forest after a rainstorm, and she fought the urge to inhale deeply while he was close to her. "Knowing other people's secrets can sometimes be a curse," she said. "But it also has its advantages."

"I can see that," Miguel responded. Gina walked a few paces behind, watching her partner with the psychic. It was early in the morning and she knew her brain might still be a little groggy, but she could swear she sensed an intimacy between those two. She made a mental note to confront Miguel about it later.

This was going to get tricky if he was dating their witness.

The small, uncooperative man from the front desk led them down a corridor to a row of rooms on the first floor that opened to a small courtyard. As was fitting with the rest of the motel, it was rundown and unkempt.

There was little doubt that there were syringes in the weed-ridden flower beds.  There was nothing inviting about this courtyard, and still Daphne's physical reaction put Miguel on edge.

"What? What is it?" he asked her.

Daphne rubbed her arms, folded across her midsection.  "I can't always stop the emotions that come flying at me, and this place... Nothing good ever happens here."

"That must be exhausting," Gina said, joining the conversation.

"It can be.  Sometimes overwhelming," Daphne answered honestly.  "But I've learned ways to control it over the years, for the most part.  Just sometimes I'm caught off guard."

"Room 33," the man announced, eyes drooping like this whole encounter was the biggest annoyance and waste of his time.  Daphne saw the teal door and the number 33 that sat in its center from her dream just a few hours ago, and she couldn't resist the chill that washed over her.  This was it.  The man opened the door and it all came rushing to her, an emotional tornado as impactful as a real gust of wind.

Fear.  And anger.  Both hit her at once.  She heard the crying that no one else could hear, felt the sting where he slapped Ellie across the face.  Daphne rubbed her own wrists, aching for an ease to the pain from the ligatures that were on the girl who'd been kept here as a prisoner.

"Is this the room you saw, Daphne?" Miguel asked, even though he knew the answer.  He could see her face and knew she was sensing something horrible.

"She was definitely here," Daphne said as she entered the room, even as the man who had opened the door for them slithered away.  Whether he just didn't care what they were doing or he didn't want to be associated with whatever was going on in the motel, Miguel had no idea.  And he didn't care.  If they had questions for him, they could hunt him down later.  Like, what was happening in room 2, for example.

The room was dark.  Only the small shafts coming from the open door and a slight opening in the curtains were bringing in any light at all.  The bedding was still rumpled.  *Good.  The room hasn't been cleaned yet.*  Grace stood at the foot of the bed.  No one could see her except Daphne, but Daphne didn't care.  She talked to her anyway.

"What do you know, Grace?" Daphne asked.

"Rick is afraid.  Kevin told him the detectives were asking about him. He took her to the Lake." Grace looked at Daphne with worried eyes.  She didn't have to say it because they both knew.  His end game happened at the Lake.

Daphne spun around to face the detectives still standing in the doorway. "He took her to the Lake."

"I believe you," Miguel said calmly.

"We need to get a forensics team in here right away. Gather as much evidence as we can," Gina stated.

Miguel nodded in agreement and then entered the room slowly.  Something had caught his eye in the middle of the ugly, dirty carpet.  He knelt at Daphne's feet.  "It's a necklace.  With the letter E on it."

"Ellie," Gina stated flatly as she pulled out her phone and called in Forensics.

"She was wearing that in my vision," Daphne explained, looking all around her at the sights that were so familiar despite the fact she'd never stepped foot in here before.  "In this very room.  In fact, that necklace is no accident.  Ellie yanked it off to leave behind."

Miguel pulled rubber gloves out of his pocket and slowly put them on, one finger at a time.  "Like breadcrumbs?"

Daphne nodded.  "Something like that."

"Does she know what Rick plans to do with her?"

Daphne exchanged a look with Grace, and Miguel let her have her moment.  A silent conversation passed between the psychic and the ghost.  "No.  Not for sure. But ever since he tied her up, she's been suspicious that it wouldn't end well."  Daphne cleared her throat.  "She doesn't know about Grace yet."

Miguel stood, and even with gloves he was careful not to touch anything. "We should get out of here. We don't want to run the risk of tampering with evidence."

Daphne followed the detective back into the courtyard where Gina was just wrapping up her call. Miguel turned suddenly and chewed his lip as if he were nervous before asking Daphne, "Does Grace know Rick's real name? Can she find out?"

Gina walked up to them, curious as well what intel they could gather from the ghost. But Daphne shook her head. "No. She only knows what he told her. She doesn't even know what high-end client bought her snuff film."

"Can she sneak in his room and take a peek at his wallet?" Miguel asked.

Daphne folded her arms across her chest. Sometimes it was like working with children. "She's not a poltergeist. She's a lost soul who needs her murderer brought to justice so she can rest peacefully in her afterlife.  Can she maybe pull off a parlor trick or two that makes him scratch his head?  Sure.  But open his wallet?  She's just a ghost."

Miguel held up his hands in innocence.  "Okay, okay.  I'm new to this.  I don't know how it all works.  I've never worked alongside my victim's spirit before."

Daphne snorted.  "That you know of."

Miguel didn't really know what to say to that, so he decided to switch gears to the other question that was on his mind.  "What kind of team do I get out here for what's being sold out of room 2?"

Daphne wagged a finger playfully at Miguel before answering, "Narcotics."

"So once the forensics team gets here, are we heading to the Lake?" Gina asked.

Miguel turned to Daphne.  "Do we know what we're looking for?"

Daphne communicated silently with Grace.  Grace had been on the boat.  She had died there.  They did have an eyewitness.  Suddenly an image flashed before her mind's eye, a white boat floating lazily on clear, gentle waters.

Daphne shook her head.  "You're not going to believe this."

Miguel looked at Gina before asking what they were both curious to know.  "Believe what?"

"The dumbass named his boat *The Born Star*." Daphne couldn't help but roll her eyes at the arrogance. "How did this guy elude law enforcement all these years?"

"Are you serious? We're looking for a boat called *The Born Star*?" Gina asked wide-eyed as Miguel immediately jumped on the phone to Spencer, his trusted tech.

Daphne nodded.  "It's white. I don't know much about boats, but it looked to be what I'd call mid-sized."

"And you believe it's at Millerton right now?" Gina probed.

"No, I *know* it is," Daphne stated with confidence.

"Then I guess I know where we're headed next."

Gina shrugged.

"I got it!" Miguel announced as he hung up his phone call. "Richard T. Belton. The boat is registered to a Richard T. Belton."

"So Rick Belton is the real Rick Bersin?" Gina raised an eyebrow.

Miguel nodded as Daphne snorted again. "This guy is really an idiot."

'I guess he used all his creative juices naming his business and couldn't go any further," Miguel stated.

"As soon as the forensics team gets here, I say we pay Rick a little visit on his *Born Star* yacht." Gina smiled. She was a lioness on the hunt, and she could sense her prey was near.

"There's just one small thing," Miguel said, and the look on his face wasn't as excited as Gina expected considering how close they were getting. "The Sarge wants to see us. Immediately."

# 11.

"The DA called," Minnie at the front desk warned Miguel and Gina as they entered the glass building downtown.  It was still early morning, but the sun was already blazing through and filling the room.  It was a beautiful architectural design, but Miguel had never understood the decision to build the façade out of windows in a place that could easily get to 110 degrees in the summertime.

"Mack," Gina stated as they realized their previous case was still looming.  Miguel, shoulders slumped, started toward the Sarge's office on the other side of the bullpen, but Gina grabbed his arm.  "I need coffee first. I can't go in there without it."

Miguel noticed that she had taken the time to put on make-up and pull her hair back neatly before meeting him at the Palm Sway early this morning, despite her coffee-less zombie state. She looked better than he did, if he was being honest. But getting up early always dragged her down and he wanted to face his tongue-lashing with his partner at full speed by his side.

He waited for Gina to fill her styrofoam cup with a splash of cream, give it a stir and sip a warm mouthful. The effect was immediate and Gina looked relieved. "Okay. Let's go."

They were halfway to his office when the Sarge noticed them. "You two. Get in here."

With only a slight bit more speed, Gina and Miguel entered his office, closing the glass door behind them. With a full wall of windows facing the bullpen there was no blocking out the prying eyes that would watch Malone and Alvarez get busted, but they could attempt to block the sound.

"Why is the District Attorney's office calling me

demanding the case files for Mack when I know that case was closed and handed over?"  Sergeant David "The Sarge" Cain was a large man, barrel-chested.  He loomed over his desk, nostrils flared, like a bull about to charge.

Gina stole a glance at Miguel before answering, "We're delivering that today.  It's all ready for them."

And Miguel quickly added, "We got sucked into this Grace Collins case."

"Which?"

"The Millerton Lake murder, sir," Miguel explained.  "We've made good headway.  Possible serial killer situation, too."

"Serial killer?" The Sarge asked skeptically.

"We don't know for sure, yet," Gina added quickly, "but the case possibly ties to other missing young girls in the area."

The Sarge stood up, anger fueling a burst of energy.  "Well, get sure.  I want a full report by end of day on this Collins case that is 'sucking you in.'  With full details on why you think you're more than a consultant in the Sheriff's jurisdiction.  And get the Mack case over to the DA.  Now.  I expect some people to be sloppy, but not you two." His nostrils flared.  For a man in charge in a law enforcement career, he wasn't really one to have a short fuse.  But he liked to keep his dirty laundry in the family, so the game changed when other offices and departments started calling.  He pointed a finger at his two detectives.  "I don't care if you have bodies piling up outside your bedroom door.  You work every case on your desk to its fullest.  And wrap it when it's wrapped so I don't get calls."

"Yes, sir.  They'll have everything before noon," Gina confirmed, squirming a bit in her chair.

The Sarge took a deep breath.  "There's always going to be another case.  Hell, there's always going to be too many cases.  There's just simply more of them than there are of us."  In his mind, Miguel agreed silently.  He always felt outnumbered on the streets of Fresno.  "But don't start slacking now," The Sarge added.

"No, sir," Miguel replied and then started to get

up, assuming the speech was over.

"About the Millerton murder," The Sarge began and Miguel froze, waiting to hear what came next.  Gina just sat and sipped her coffee.  "How do we know there is a tie to other cases?"

"We have an informant," Miguel said quickly.  Too quickly.  He was afraid Gina might be a bit too honest in her response and mention the fact they were working with a psychic.  Perhaps he was still afraid he was going crazy, but he wasn't ready to divulge that piece of information to the boss man just yet.

"And it's still too soon to connect all the dots," Gina added, giving Miguel a side eye.  "But we had a tip that the murderer stayed at the Palm Sway recently and there was evidence that he's taken another girl.  Our vic's best friend.  Kidnapping happened in Fresno, so it *is* Fresno P.D. jurisdiction. Forensics is out there now."

The Sarge rubbed his chin and Miguel held his breath waiting for some kind of reaction.  This morning he'd felt so confident in this case.  In fact, he'd been buoyant with the energy that came from the things that were falling into place.  But now, hearing the details out loud, it suddenly felt flimsy at best.

"We haven't had a serial killer in a long time," The Sarge finally said.  "Get with P.R.  We don't need a press nightmare on our hands.  Or worse yet, the Fresno Bee tipping our suspect's hand.  Do we have a suspect?"

"We have two persons of interest.  Kevin Kyle and Rick Belton, also goes by Rick Bersin.  All connected to a film company called *The Born Stars*," Miguel explained, still with trepidation, as he felt he was dancing on a wire.

The Sarge wrinkled his large brow and folded his heavy arms.  "Good work.  Give me the full report later.  Make sure the Sheriff's Department is aware of what you'll be handling so we don't have any jurisdiction pissing matches."

Miguel exhaled with relief and waited for Gina to join him in standing before heading toward the glass door.

"And Alvarez," The Sarge shouted over his

shoulder. "Go clean up. You look like shit." Gina laughed heartily as she and Miguel exited the office and walked back to their desks.

Miguel started to login to his computer as Gina said, "He's not used to seeing you not completely put together."

"I'm put together," Miguel mumbled defensively, but there was no fervor behind his words.

"Wrinkled shirt, hair not perfectly styled. Who is this man and what has he done with my partner?" Gina lifted the files for the Mack case.

Miguel shook his head. "There *is* something about this Collins case that has me knocked off my game."

"I noticed," Gina smirked. "She's perky and blonde. Oh—and she talks to ghosts. Is that a quality you were looking for in a woman?"

"Shut up." Miguel laughed as he spoke. He couldn't really deny it, could he? Part of his distraction was Daphne.

"Hey, I've been telling you to start dating for years now.  If you ask me, this is exactly what you've been needing."

"She's just helping us on our case," Miguel responded, again half-heartedly.  He knew Gina would see right through him, and the look on her face told him she did, but he couldn't tell her how he thought his soul was somehow connected to Daphne's.  It had been hard enough to admit that he was starting to believe Daphne was really talking to Grace Collins.

"Yeah, yeah.  Let's drop these files off and then head to Millerton.  Are we bringing Daphne with us?"

"I don't think we need to risk her safety," Miguel replied.

"The woman talks to ghosts for a living.  I don't think you need to protect her sensibilities."

"Oh, thank God, you guys are here."  Spencer came up to Miguel's desk.  He was slightly out of breath and distinctly more disheveled than Miguel.  He looked like he might have spent the night at his keyboard.  And he honestly might have—he'd done it before.  His hoodie sweatshirt was unzipped, revealing a wrinkled white tee beneath.  His long, shaggy hair went every which way into the air and down across his face.  "After you had me check the registration on that boat, I got a little curious.  I know you didn't ask me to, but I cross-referenced the Richard Belton guy against last known whereabouts in the missing persons database."  Spencer smiled a devious smile.

"You got a hit."  Gina filled in the blank.

"Detective Malone," Spencer said, leaning in conspiratorially, "I got six hits."

"What?" Miguel asked, surprise and excitement really invigorating him.  He had the case-coming-together energy again.  But he knew now their hunch had been right all along.  They were going to need to find Ellie and tie this guy to other cases in the process.  He wasn't going to go down for one murder, but for many.

Spencer dropped a printout on Miguel's desk.  "He used a credit card within one square mile of *every* one of these missing girls' last known locations."

"What's the address on file for that credit card?" Miguel asked.

"Why, I'm glad you asked, Mikey," Spencer gloated, and pulled out another piece of paper he laid on Miguel's desk. "He lives out by Van Ness Extension."

"Of course, he does," Miguel mumbled as he checked the address sitting on his desk. That was a fancy part of town, opposite direction from Kevin Kyle, but also swanky and posh.

"I'll get us a warrant to check Belton's house, but we need to get out to Millerton. Now." Gina stared hard at Miguel. He knew that look. She was nervous they were running out of time. And they still had to wrap the Mack case before they were both fired.

"Spencer, have I told you you're the best?" Miguel nodded at the tech as he grabbed his keys to show Gina he understood—and agreed with—her urgency. There was little doubt now that this guy was behind multiple disappearances and one confirmed murder.

And he had Ellie.

"You can't live without me," Spencer smiled as he started to stroll back to his desk.

But something was bouncing around Miguel's mind. A part of the case that wasn't falling into place as easily. It nagged at his brain even though he couldn't make the pieces fit. "And, Spencer?"

Spencer turned around and raised an eyebrow. "Yeah?"

"Start looking for connections for Kevin Kyle too. He's involved somehow. I just can't put my finger on it."

Spencer nodded. "Baby stuff."

Gina nudged Miguel. "Let's go." He felt it too. They should have already been at Millerton by now, but the new case had so distracted them from the previous one. And now Ellie was paying the price for their delay.

Gina and Miguel headed toward the front glass façade when Miguel's phone rang.

"Detective Alvarez," he answered, but continued

toward the front.  Gina wouldn't have let him stop even if he'd wanted to.

"Detective, it's Daphne."

Her voice both warmed him and chilled him at the same time.  She wasn't much of a chitchatter, so he sensed she had something to share.

"Whatcha got for me, Daph?"  After he'd called her by the nickname that he'd had no idea would come out of his mouth, he cringed at himself for being so casual with a witness.  He needed to pull himself together when it came to Daphne Winters.

"We're too late.  They're not at the boat anymore."  Daphne's voice was heavy. And it sunk Miguel's heart like a stone.

"Well. Shit."

# 12.

Daphne paced her living room, the ghost of the young, blonde girl hovering in the corner.

Daphne gestured wildly to Grace. "How is he always one step ahead?  He can't possibly know you're working with the police."

Grace shook her head.  "He knows nothing.  This is just Ellie's movie.  Rick will film whatever he gets paid to film."

"How did you ever get caught up with a guy like that in the first place?"

Grace's ghost shrugged.  "I was young and naïve. He came into the ice cream shop where I worked.  Told me I was pretty, that he directed films and I'd be perfect.

I was sucked into the lie with false dreams of making it big."

Daphne groaned. "What a hunk of crap that guy is."

"The worst part is, I sucked Ellie into it.  That's why we have to save her. If he hurts her, it's my fault."

"If he hurts her, it's because he's a piece of shit human being.  It's not your fault.  It's no accident that he preys on young, naïve girls.  You're a victim here, too." Daphne flopped on her armchair by the front window, suddenly feeling completely overcome by exhaustion.  It wasn't just Grace and Ellie, it was all the cases she'd worked over the years, starting with when she was a child.  Helping spirits was part of who she was, she couldn't just run from it. But some days... Some days she really just wanted to find a quiet place where ghosts couldn't find her so she could hide out for a few.

It was part of the reason she had moved to Fresno.  And look where it had gotten her.

Daphne was well aware that her feelings and

emotions were projected out just as the spirit's projected back to her, so it came as no surprise when Grace softened toward Daphne. She spoke low, her disembodied voice barely more than a whisper in the wind. "You don't make enough time for yourself."

"Murderers don't take time off, so neither do I."

"But it's not your responsibility to save everyone. Some of us can't be saved."

Daphne looked up at the ghost in her living room, the young girl no one else could see. Grace had a haunted look that went far beyond the echoes of death. And even as she might be tired and ready to hide again, Daphne knew she couldn't abandon her. Daphne knew with clarity as sharp as a knife that Grace's unfinished business had nothing to do with Rick Belton, and everything to do with her best friend. Her spirit couldn't rest until Ellie was saved. That just upped the ante a bit.

Daphne spoke as softly as Grace had. "Saving a life and saving a soul are two different things. And I won't rest until I do both for you and Ellie."

A knock at the door interrupted their conversation. Daphne hopped out of the chair and bounced to the door. She couldn't help but feel better that the detectives were there. She opened the door and Miguel stood alone on her doorstep. She was surprised, but not sad. This was the detective she needed the most anyway.

"Can I come in?" His brown eyes were heavy, sad. She realized in an instant that he carried the same weight she did, just in a different way.

Daphne stepped aside and held the door open. "Of course."

"Is Grace here?" He looked around the living room, as if he'd be able to tell with his eyes. He couldn't.

"She is. She's worried about Ellie."

"Tell him about the warehouse," Grace blurted to Daphne.

"I..." Miguel looked at the ground as if he were embarrassed and then back up at Daphne's eyes. Daphne was surprised to feel emotional when he looked at her that way—so vulnerable.  "I wanted to ask her some questions.  Is that okay?"

Daphne looked at Grace and she nodded.  "Go for it."

"Have you ever done anything like that before?" Miguel asked, a weird look of skepticism flashing across his face.

Daphne smiled.  A genuine smile.  "You might be surprised.  And, also, she wants you to know that they've taken Ellie to a warehouse that Rick sometimes uses for his films.  We think he filmed some on the boat, but whatever he has to film next he needed indoors."

"We were actually on our way to Millerton," Miguel said.  "But we can seize the boat later looking for evidence.  Does she know where the warehouse is?"

Daphne shook her head.  "Industrial area of town."

"Okay, we'll find it."  Miguel fished a photo out of his pocket and swung his arm left to right, not really knowing where Grace was.  "Does she know who this guy is?"

Daphne froze his arm and then positioned it toward Grace's spirit. In an instant, Grace disappeared and reappeared an inch from the photo. Her eyes bulged at the image and excited energy filled the room. "That's the guy who killed me. He wore a ski mask for the video but I know it was him. It was only me, Rick and Kyle on the boat. And Kyle had the knife."

"I thought Rick killed you?" Daphne answered while Miguel frantically fought his curiosity to know what was going on.

"Rick was complicit but no, he filmed it all. This guy—" She pointed at the photo and it fluttered gently from the force. "This guy slashed my throat and dumped me overboard into the lake."

"She says this guy's name is Kyle and that he's the one who actually ended her life while Rick filmed for his shitty movie," Daphne translated for Miguel.

"What?" Miguel couldn't hide his shock at this interesting piece of information. He'd known Kyle was involved somehow, but he was the actual killer? "Why did she tell her mother Rick was the murderer?"

"Rick is the one who lured her, built her trust and betrayed her, so she blames him more. But this guy and Rick are in cahoots," Daphne explained.

"I'll have my team find the warehouse. This ends today," Miguel stated as he tucked the photo back in his pocket. "Between the toothbrush found in the Palm Sway room and whatever evidence we uncover on his boat, there's no way we can't lock these two up for a very long time. Tell Grace thank you."

"She heard you." Daphne smiled again. Miguel found that he liked seeing her smile. It didn't seem like something she did very often.

"I'm going to go be with Ellie, Daphne. Will you be okay?" Grace asked, her ghostly eyes soft.

"Yeah. Go to her. We'll meet you there," Daphne responded. And, as if on cue, Grace was gone.

"You've been a tremendous help to the case, Daphne, but I don't think you should come," Miguel explained.  "Let the Police Department handle it from here."

"I don't think so.  I'm coming."

"These guys are callous, probably armed and dangerous.  They've already proven they have no qualms about killing anyone."

"I promised Grace, so I'll be there when you save Ellie."  Daphne folded her arms defiantly.  Truth be told, she was a little hurt that he hadn't seen her as part of his team, the way Cayman always had.

"You can't make promises to ghosts."  Miguel raised his voice, the words flying out before he thought them through.

"I made a promise to a young girl who has been greatly wronged by the world of the living.  Yes, she happens to be a ghost, but that makes no difference to me.  And it shouldn't to you either."  Daphne raised her voice right back.  She'd gone toe to toe with plenty of people who'd underestimated her before, she just didn't think she should be doing it with Miguel.  "Whether you can sense them or not, the ghosts of all your victims weigh on you, too."

Miguel froze, unable to respond.  Because she was right.

He swallowed hard and looked at Daphne's face. Her hair was unkempt, as if she'd gone to great lengths to look disheveled.  She had hard lines on her face from the years of dealing with death, kidnappings and murder. She was tense in her shoulders, coiled and ready to strike, always wanting to draw first blood lest anyone dig too deep and see that underneath it all she was just a frightened human being who cared too much in a world that never seemed to care at all.

She was just like him.

He regretted it two seconds after he did it, but he grabbed Daphne's shoulders, leaned in and pressed his lips to hers.  He wished his kiss could ease her burden, erasing all the cases that never closed, deafening the roar of ghosts only she could hear.  But he knew this might have the opposite effect, and so he backed away with remorse in his eyes.  He wasn't completely remorseful, as the kiss seemed to complete something in him like a puzzle piece that slips into its place.  But he had a twinge of regret that he might have overstepped his boundaries and needlessly complicated things.

"I'm sorry."   He said the words that were supposed to undo the hands of time on any regret, but instead just sounded hollow and weak.

Daphne simply shrugged.  "Don't be.  You can't fight it any more than I can.  Our souls are linked."

"So what does that mean?"   Miguel truly wondered.  He couldn't deny there was *something* pulling him in.

"I'm not completely sure.  It's never happened to me before, but many cultures believe certain souls are always together before, during and after life.  Those souls are always seeking each other out even when we're not aware of it consciously."

"Like a soul mate?"

"I guess, kinda."

Miguel huffed a laugh.  "That's ridiculous."

"Hard to believe, right?"

Miguel nodded.  He didn't believe in soul mates and souls linked in the afterlife.  "Yeah."

Daphne raised an eyebrow.  "Kinda like the ghost of your victim directing you to the location of her murderer?"

Miguel smirked at Daphne's sarcasm.  "You can rest your case, councilor."

"I don't know what to tell you, Miguel.  I mean, Detective Alvarez," Daphne corrected, chastising herself for being so forward.

"I think we're past formalities, don't you?"

"Let me grab my phone and we should head out to that warehouse.  Ellie's minutes are precious," Daphne stated.  Partially she wanted this conversation to be over with, and partially she really *did* feel a sense of urgency for Ellie.  "And, Miguel?"

He looked at her questioningly, but it was so endearing she almost grabbed him and kissed him herself.  "I've felt it too.  The pull we have."  She gestured between the two of them.  "I guess what I'm trying to say is, I liked it."

She smiled a half smile and she shoved her phone in her pocket and led Miguel out the front door of her apartment.

Ghosts.  Murder.  False identities.  And now a psychic might be his soul mate?  Things were getting really complicated for Miguel.  He liked neat and tidy.  Organized and by the book.  Daphne had entered his world and blown all that to pieces.

And he surprised himself again when he realized it didn't bother him at all.  In fact, he kinda liked it.

# 13.

Ellie sat in the dark, her hands tied behind her back, her feet bound at the ankles.  Her eyes were dry— she was way past crying or panic.  After multiple failed attempts at escaping, she'd resolved herself to whatever fate lay ahead.

The same fate as Grace, she presumed.

What kind of movies did this Born Stars film company make?  One where you had to kidnap teenagers? It didn't make any sense.

And what *had* happened to Grace?  Was she still gagged and bound somewhere?  Human trafficked? Dead?  Ellie felt very alone, and it wasn't just because Rick and Kyle had left her here in the dark.  Her parents wouldn't even miss her for days.  She'd always told herself she was the lucky one.  Other parents kept close ties on their kids, wanting to know their every movement.  Ellie's parents had always been free with her, encouraging independence.

But now she wondered if maybe it was because they just didn't really care.  Maybe they just liked her being out of their hair so they could start enjoying their empty nest years while their daughter was still a minor.

Life was ironic.  And cruel.

A scratching sound put her senses on high alert.  She stared into the black abyss, ears perked for more auditory evidence. Silence.

And then a soft sound like a light footstep.  Someone was coming her way.

"Who's there?" Ellie called out.  She felt stupid as soon as she did, but then at least the approacher knew she knew they were there.  Ellie tensed, bracing for the moment she'd been dreading.  Her heart was thumping loudly in her chest and fresh tears threatened to spring from her eyes again.  She was tied up and helpless.

And someone was coming.

Hopefully they ended it all quickly.  She would face death as bravely as she could.  But torture might be harder.  She hoped it wasn't going to be slow and drawn out, all filmed for some psycho's pleasure.

The footsteps were maybe ten feet in front of her.  But even acclimated to the dark as she was, she couldn't see anything.  Not even a rough form of the person to know if he were tall or short, strong or skinny.

"I know you're there.  And whatever you do to me, I'm going to fight you to the end," Ellie shouted into the void with a fake bravado.  If she made it tough on them, would they let her go?  She doubted it.  They'd probably like it more.

A breeze flittered past Ellie's face, forcing her hair to rise and fall with its momentum.  She saw nothing but could feel his closeness.  She squeezed her eyes shut tight, no longer brave enough to face the oncoming blow.

A thump behind her and she turned her head as

far she could.  She still saw nothing.  Losing her sight was frustrating her.  She didn't want to see, but somehow because she couldn't see, it made it all the more maddening.

"What do you want?" Ellie shouted.

Her hair fluttered again as a soft whisper danced across her ear.  "Ellie."

She knew that voice.  "Grace?"

Silence.

"Grace, is that you?  I can't see you.  I can't see anything."

Suddenly, a small lamp on a table next to Ellie lit up.  It was a soft glow, but enough to light up the area all around her.  She felt goosebumps rise as her eyes confirmed that no one was there.  How had the light turned on?

Ellie breathed shallow breaths, a rising panic filling her chest.  Being tied up and left in a dark room was one thing, but then the mind games too?  It was too much.

"Ellie. I'm here."  Again, Grace's voice fluttered softly near her ear.

"Grace?" This was it.  She had snapped and was now hearing imaginary voices to keep her company in captivity.  Fine.  She'd play along.  It was better than wasting away in the darkness. But then... Someone had turned the lamp on.

"Hang on, Ellie.  You're almost free."

The voice was so soft it was like a fragile butterfly's wing.  But Ellie wanted it to be real so badly. So she hung on to the thin fiber of faith.  Somehow, real or imagined, Grace was here with her.  Ellie swallowed the emotion filling up in her throat.  "Don't leave me, Gracie.  I'm scared."

"Help is coming."

Her mind was a tangle of thoughts and worries. She didn't know what was real and what was delusion. But she found that she didn't care anymore.  What was left of her hope was dangling by a very thin thread.  If the imaginary voice of Grace said help was coming, then she would believe it.  What else did she have to hold on to?

"Help is coming," Ellie repeated.

# 14.

"This is the address on file," Miguel explained as he strapped on his bullet proof vest. Gina next to him did the same. He turned to Daphne. "Stay by the car until we give the all-clear."

Daphne nodded. With anyone else she would've flipped him off and done whatever the hell she wanted to do, but not with Miguel. She knew unequivocally that he was just protecting her. That he said the words as much for his own sake as for hers. So she would wait by the car until they had Ellie.

At the end of the day, that was all that mattered.

A line of SWAT team members readied at various entry points. Daphne had never seen anything like it.

She knew they had no idea what waited for them on the other side of the warehouse doors—a violent battle to the death or darkness and emptiness.  And they were going to go in anyway.

A man in a suit seemed to be giving the orders, and he made some gesture that appeared to be the go-ahead.  Like an explosion, every SWAT team member stationed at every door readied their weapons and burst into the warehouse.

Silence then followed.

Miguel nodded at Gina and a wordless exchange passed between them.

Before they headed to the building, Miguel glanced back at Daphne one last time.  She smiled.  She wasn't worried at all because she knew it was only Ellie and Grace inside—something the SWAT team would soon discover.

Guns drawn, Miguel and Gina slowly approached the side door to the warehouse.  It was painted gray against a white building, and for some reason to Daphne that felt like it meant something.  Just before Miguel entered, there was a loud, strong voice giving the all-clear.  Miguel and Gina ran in.

The overhead lights were on inside the building now, and Ellie had to blink to adjust to the sharp contrast. But after the initial fear that had overtaken her when armed men stormed the building, she realized these were the good guys and she was being rescued.  Her shoulders racked with sobs as the relief, fear, elation, all exploded in an overwhelming emotional release.  She was going home.

"Detectives. Over here."  A man dressed all in black called Miguel and Gina over to the bed where Ellie was tied up.

Miguel knelt at the bed as the man untied her ligatures.  He studied her face a bit, looking for signs of serious injury.  She looked dirty and had a large bruise across her face, but otherwise she appeared to be unharmed.

"I'm Detective Malone. This is Detective Alvarez,

Ellie," Gina stated, securing her gun near the young girl. "You're safe now."

"Are you hurt?" Miguel asked calmly, keeping the frustrated anger simmering just below the surface.  He was happy they'd found Ellie, but the manhunt for the two Born Star killers was just getting started.

Through sobs and a tear-stained face, the teenage girl shook her head.

Gina sat on the bed and pulled the girl near. "There's an ambulance here.  They're going to check you out just to be safe, okay?"  The girl nodded.

The man in black told Miguel and Gina, "All clear. No perps were found in or around the building."

Through emotional sniffs and a tight throat, Ellie managed to say, "They left me here in the dark a while ago.  I don't know where they went."

"We're going to find them.  Every cop in Fresno is looking for them.  Sheriff out at the lake too. They'll pay for kidnapping you and murdering Grace."  Miguel spoke with a firm, committed voice.

Ellie whispered to herself, "So, it was her ghost."

"Grace was here with you, wasn't she?" came an unexpected female voice. "You weren't completely alone in the dark."

Miguel turned to see Daphne standing there, leaning into one hip, her long skirt swaying with the motion.

Miguel stood up. "I thought you were going to wait outside."

Daphne shrugged. "I knew Rick and Kyle weren't here all along. I just didn't want you to worry. I also knew Grace was here with Ellie." Daphne looked around. "But she's not here now."

"I think she left when the SWAT team arrived." Ellie looked up at Daphne. Her whole ordeal with the kidnappers had been way more traumatic than hanging out with a ghost. Daphne sensed she would approach the supernatural and afterlife with a completely different attitude after all this. Naturally, people tend to be skeptical or afraid of what they can't see and explain. But for Ellie, her dead friend's ghost had been a comfort in a time of need.  She now knew what Daphne knew about spirits, and the club of believers, always small and exclusive, had grown by one.

Gina helped Ellie to stand.  "Let me take you to the ambulance."

Miguel turned to Daphne as Gina escorted Ellie outside of the warehouse.  "Where did she go?"

"Beats me."  Daphne shrugged again, nonchalant.

Miguel raised an eyebrow.  "But you always know all kinds of random things.  You can't open up your senses and ask the universe or something?"

Daphne smirked.  She had met so few people in her life like herself and nobody else could possibly understand the world as psychics saw it.  "It doesn't really work like that.  It's more like intuition on a magnified scale.  But my instinct with Grace is that she went wherever Rick is."

"Great.  Can you ask her for an address?"

Daphne shook her head.  "No one wants Rick

punished more than Grace, trust me.  She'll be back with whatever information she can get."

"Miguel!" Gina called from the side door of the warehouse.  "The warrant for the Born Star boat just came through.  Let's go."

Miguel hesitated for a moment.

Daphne shooed him with her hands.  "Go.  Do your job.  And I'll do mine."

# 15.

Ellie sat on the edge of the back of the ambulance, a blanket wrapped around her shoulders. Daphne approached purposefully.  She didn't need to touch her, but it was better to have eye contact and to be near when she did her reading.

"So, they only filmed one scene so far.  On the boat?" Daphne asked, although she already knew the answer.

"I guess that's what it was.  They'd told me they were making a music video, but it was so weird."  Ellie shook her head at the memory, her shoulders slumped with the emotional exhaustion of all she'd been through.

Daphne held her hands out in front of Ellie,

feeling her energy.  Ellie had never seen anyone do that before.

"What are you doing?" Ellie asked.  There was no judgment in the question, just curiosity.

"I'm psychic," Daphne said, as if that explained everything.  Ellie watched her for a moment as Daphne pulled what information she could from her senses.

"Is that how you knew Grace was here with me?" Ellie asked through soft, brown eyes.

Daphne nodded.  "It's also how I know that it's not your fault.  Rick and Kyle prey on teenage girls like you and Grace.  *They're* the assholes.  You have survivor's guilt.  I see it a lot."

Ellie looked away, as if the truths that Daphne was reflecting back to her were too painful to face.  Daphne didn't force her. She knew the roller coaster that was going on inside Ellie's mind and heart.

"You're a victim too," Daphne said softly.

"But I'm still alive."  Ellie's voice was soft, but flat. She simply stated facts.  "I'm barely even hurt.  But Grace is *dead.*"

Daphne sat on the edge of the ambulance next to Ellie.  She'd never been much of a sugar-coater so she didn't see any reason to start now.  "There are different kinds of pain, ya know.  And I deal with the dead all the time.  Grace's okay.  And you'll be okay too.  This might seem strange to say, but maybe this was something you needed."

Ellie didn't argue, but she did ask, "Okay...?"

"You were sixteen going on forty.  Running around acting like you knew it all.  Maybe now you'll take the time to appreciate things."

Ellie nodded.  "Yes.  I think I will."

"I'm trying to pick through your memories to find something that might tell me where Rick and Kyle are.  We need to find them before they do something to hurt someone else."

"They were going to kill me, too, weren't they?" Again, Ellie's voice was soft, but there was no panic or overwrought emotion.

Daphne nodded. "Most likely. They make snuff films, not music videos.  You know what those are? Where people die on film?"

"Who would pay for that?"

Daphne curled her lip at the thought of the type of person who would pay for a snuff film.  This was why she preferred the dead to the living.  Spirits never cared about material goods or using people to improve their own stations.  They were way past all that.  "I think the world is full of garbage people.  But that makes it all the more special when you meet someone truly good.  And I'm guessing now you'll be better than most at spotting the difference."

Miguel's face flashed into her mind for just a moment.

"I don't know where they went, but I did hear them talking about an investor.  Some kind of business meeting," Ellie explained.

Daphne opened her mind's eye and a flash of a restaurant popped into her vision.  There were white tablecloths, waiters dressed to the nines, water goblets…definitely not the type of place Daphne frequented. She'd have to start looking for fancy restaurants.

A female EMT walked over to Daphne and Ellie. "We're heading to the hospital now, Ellie," she said. "Your vitals are good, but it's just a formality. Your parents will meet you there."

Ellie looked at Daphne with a puzzled expression, and Daphne knew exactly what it was all about. Her parents had never even cared what she did or where she did it before. Were they worried?

Daphne answered her look with, "Maybe they learned something today, too." Daphne hopped down from the edge of the ambulance so the EMT could help Ellie go deeper inside.

Ellie stood, but she remained looking at Daphne. "Thank you. And please tell Grace something for me."

"Of course."

"Tell her, 'You win.' She'll know what it means."

Daphne simply nodded and the ambulance doors closed.  At least Ellie was safe.  But now to find the bastards who took her.  And somehow she thought she might have a pretty good idea of who might be able to tell her.

# 16.

"They didn't even attempt to hide their tracks." Gina held up a box of clear DVD cases with unmarked discs inside them. "Why does this seem so old school?"

Miguel lifted one of the discs with a gloved finger. "Probably can't stream snuff films on Netflix."

"Hey, Alvarez, Malone." Officer Long called them over with a wave of her hand. "Check out this treasure trove." She lifted the lid to a small shoebox that made no sense tucked away on a boat. Inside the box were bracelets, rings, necklaces, small shiny trinkets of every style and color.

"What the...?" Miguel started.

Gina rolled her eyes. "Keepsakes. From their

victims."

"These guys are going down when we match these to missing girls.  We'll be able to tie them to a lot more cases than just Grace and Ellie."  With a gloved hand, Miguel lifted a couple of the necklaces, inspecting them, wondering who they belonged to.  Many a family would be thankful to have the jewelry back and the closure on their missing daughter.  Miguel was suddenly overwhelmed by the thought that there was even a market for these types of films in the first place.  All these girls lost their lives so some sickos could get their jollies.

Gina shook her head.  "Something about this doesn't seem right.  It's too easy."

"You get away with something for long enough and you start to think you always will."  Miguel squinted at Gina, the bright sun reflecting off the box of jewelry.  The boat swayed beneath their feet and a silent exchange passed between them.

"What if this is bigger than Rick and Kyle?"  Gina spoke her thoughts softly to her partner.

"You think all this evidence was planted to have these guys take the full fall?"

"I don't know what I think."  Gina braced herself as the boat pitched a bit.  "Just doesn't make sense to me yet.  These guys murder this many girls—"  She gestured at the pile of jewelry in the box.  "—and go undetected for years, and yet they aren't even trying to evade anything.  They leave evidence on the very boat where it all took place. Registered in their own name."

"Cocky or stupid," Miguel responded.

"Or maybe more?" Gina cocked an eyebrow.

"We've got blood for sure."  David, the forensic scientist, walked over to the detectives.  "We'll get samples over to the lab to confirm DNA matches."

"Enough to be a murder scene?" Gina asked.  A few drops of blood on a boat could be anything.  A good defense attorney could easily cast reasonable doubt with a jury.  You could cut yourself cleaning a fish, lifting heavy equipment, something sharp on the floor...they were good at coming up with alternative scenarios to explain away solid evidence.  Gina had seen it done too many times in her career.

"Oh, yeah."  David pointed to the front of the boat.  "They tried to clean it up but did a poor job. There's splatter consistent with a violent attack and pools on the cushions and floor."

"Splatter that could come from a throat being slit?" Miguel asked, thinking of Grace.

David nodded.  "That would do it for sure.  Throat wounds bleed heavily."

"Bastards," Miguel swore under his breath.  He hated those two cocky murderers in that moment.

"How long will it take for you to confirm a DNA match with Grace?" Gina asked.

"We can expedite and get it back in a couple of days," David confirmed.

Gina nodded and the forensic scientist went back to work.  Gina and Miguel climbed off the boat onto the dock, removing their gloves once they were safely on sturdy ground.

"We have enough to at least bring these two assholes in," Miguel stated.

"We've got them on the kidnapping charge at the very least," Gina agreed.  "But we need to act quickly. They could run when they realize we freed Ellie."

"We need to get what we have to the D.A. as soon as possible," Miguel said to Gina. Then he turned over his shoulder to talk to Officer Long, still on the boat. "We need positive ID's for both the girls on those DVDs and-or their jewelry ASAP.  Cross-reference to the missing persons list we already pulled."

"I'm on it," Officer Long confirmed.

"You realize if you're right and there is more to this case, Kyle and Rick are just the steppingstones." Miguel squinted at Gina.  It was already starting to be a warm, sunny California day.

"I hope I'm wrong and these two were just sloppy, but..."  Gina shook her head.

"But what?"

"But I have a funny feeling I'm right."

Miguel cocked an eyebrow at Gina.  "Well, what's the good of working with a psychic and a ghost if we don't use them?"

"Are you suggesting we put Grace's ghost to work?"

"That's exactly what I'm saying.  Hell, if she hadn't gone to Daphne in the first place, I don't know what we'd have," Miguel said.  He started walking down the dock back toward their cars.  Gina was close on his heels.

"I'm proud of you, Miguel," Gina smiled.  "From closed-door skeptic to embracing the supernatural in a matter of days."

Miguel stopped at the car, smiling at Gina over the hood.  "We've had anonymous sources before."

"You know I'm game.  Perhaps all these years when you've heard really successful detectives and FBI agents say their victims talk to them, they weren't speaking metaphorically."

"I don't know why I spent so much time resisting.

It sure does make our job a lot easier." Miguel climbed in and started the engine. Gina climbed in the passenger seat seconds after.

"I wonder how much time we have?" Gina asked.

"How do you mean?" Miguel backed up and pulled onto the dirt road that led them to the main road from the lake.

"Well, ghosts stick around for unfinished business, right?"

"How the hell should I know?"

"At some point, Grace's business will be finished and she'll cross over. If Ellie was her unfinished business, we may not have much time with her left."

Miguel rubbed his chin and thought about it for a second. "I guess there's no sense in speculating. Once we finish with the D.A., we can head to Daphne and ask her."

"And if Grace is still around, we need to get her searching for the Born Stars sugar daddy right away."

Miguel nodded and pulled out onto the winding

road that would lead them back out of the foothills and into the city of Fresno.  He frowned a bit to himself thinking about the bizarre twists of this case that had led them to using his victim's ghost as an informant.  It certainly wouldn't be admissible in court.

But Miguel was finding he didn't care.  He wanted answers and any lead was a good lead, wasn't it?

# 17.

Mrs. Collins was vacuuming and humming gently to herself.  It helped her to stay busy—kept her mind off the horrible thoughts that crept in when she thought about Grace and how she suffered at the end.  When she let herself go to dark places in her mind, Mrs. Collins would chastise herself for not protecting her daughter more fiercely.  But how on earth could she have known?

She never liked that Rick, but the thought of murder had never entered her mind.  And now her baby had paid the price.

So she vacuumed every square inch of the house—even moving furniture to find spots to clean that hadn't seen the sun in years.  The dust bunnies that had collected behind the dining hutch had been particularly overwhelming in their infestation.  It felt cathartic to suck them up with the vacuum cleaner, erasing the painful past they represented.  And even when no trace was left, Mrs. Collins continued to clean the same spot because it eased her soul and her aching heart.

"Mom?"

The voice was so soft, Mrs. Collins swore she felt it more than heard it.

She turned off the vacuum cleaner so her hearing wouldn't be obstructed.  A glance all around the room told her eyes no one was there.  She was hearing phantom voices now.  She turned the vacuum back on and fought the tears that threatened to burst forth.  She *wanted* to hear phantom voices.  She *wanted* Grace to come visit her one last time. These tricks of the mind were cruel and they tore open the wound in her heart with a forceful jerk.

So she vacuumed the same spot she'd been vacuuming for at least ten minutes.  The carpet and the baseboard were clear of any debris.  But she didn't care. She would clean until her back ached and her shoulder throbbed so it could distract her from the deep pain in her soul.

And then suddenly the vacuum stopped.  Mrs. Collins looked to see the plug yanked out of the wall.  Had she been vacuuming that forcefully?  Or could it be…?

She dared to voice what her heart had been foolishly hoping.  "Grace?"

"Hi, mom."

Mrs. Collins looked all around the room.  There was nothing.  But she *heard* her voice.  "I can't see you."

Silence was the response.  Had she imagined it? She couldn't let go of the tiniest glimmer of hope that Grace's soul was there with her in the room.  She knew it was possible ever since she had the dream where Grace had visited her.  Without a doubt, that had been more than a dream.  It had been a visitation—and she knew it.

And somehow she didn't care that she couldn't hold her baby.  She was comforted to have her near in whatever capacity she could take at this moment. "Gracie. Just let me see you one last time."

"Get out."

Grace's voice was faint and her words didn't make sense, so Mrs. Collins struggled to believe she was hearing everything correctly. "What?"

A pad of paper sat on the counter, where Mrs. Collins had always kept it so that everyone in the family could write each other messages. She watched as the connected pen lifted and words slowly began to appear on the pad. GET OUT.

Mrs. Collins began to breathe heavily. Was this really an evil spirit using her pain with Grace to scare her? Because it was working. Or maybe...it was simply Grace with a warning?

It didn't matter.

Before she could process the words, or the supernatural event that had taken place in her home, someone snuck up behind Mrs. Collins and hit her hard in the back of the head.

The world went black.

And Grace screamed—although no one in the land of the living could hear it.

# 18.

"Pin the evidence on them and cut them loose. We have other issues right now," the heavyset man said. She couldn't see either man very well, but Daphne knew these two were the masterminds in the whole plot. She struggled to make the vision clear, but she couldn't. "We need to move the merchandise. And keep it clean."

She just knew enough to know there was a hierarchy here and these two men had successfully evaded the law for a long time by "keeping it clean." And she also knew that their version of clean and hers were vastly different. They just meant make sure it couldn't come back to them.

The harder Daphne pushed on the vision, to see a

face or anything identifiable, the more the vision pulled away.  It was so frustrating.  She needed Grace.  Talking to ghosts was always easier for her and she could get direct information.

But she didn't have Grace at the moment, so she turned to the only other person she seemed to think about these days.

"Something's wrong," Daphne told Miguel over the phone.  "Can you come by?"

"Yeah.  I had planned to after we hand the case over to the District Attorney's office.  We found so much evidence on that boat," Miguel explained.  His voice was filled with the emotional high that came from stopping someone who thought they were immune from law and order.

"Oh, I know.  Those guys are buffoons.  I'm impressed there wasn't a letter written in crayon that said, 'We did it.'"  Daphne rolled her eyes, although Miguel couldn't see it.

Her reaction piqued Miguel's interest.  "So you

sound like you believe there's more to this story?"  He remembered Gina's words—and had planned to bring it up with Daphne later anyway.

"There is.  I'll see you in a bit."  Daphne hung up the phone without a good-bye and then thought perhaps she'd been too rash.  Pleasantries and niceties had always annoyed her—social norms that required you to act a certain way, that was all bullshit.  But something about Miguel made her regret that part of her personality.  Like maybe he deserved her at least making the effort or something.  She shrugged to herself.

She hadn't seen Grace since the warehouse, so she didn't have details—only feelings.  But she had sensed Grace's anguish and her fears were getting the best of her.  Something told her it wasn't another missing girl, but it was something along those lines.  She could feel it, but capturing the details kept escaping her.  It was like watching a movie out of your peripheral vision, but as soon as you actually turned toward the screen, the movie would stop and the screen would go black.

"Grace, where are you?" Daphne called out.  She just wanted to ask her some questions.  But Grace didn't reappear so Daphne had no choice but to wait.  Wait for Grace.  Wait for Miguel.

Daphne hated waiting.

She sat in the armchair in her living room for a few minutes, but her energy turned restless.  So she stood and began pacing.  But that was getting her nowhere, so she asked herself what would Duncan and Duane do—her old team from the Paranormal Investigators League?

She hated to admit it, but she knew what they would do.  When they didn't have her to communicate directly with the entity in a particular haunting, they turned to good old-fashioned research.  Yuck.  But Daphne had nothing better to do, so she walked over to the old table she used as a desk near her small apartment kitchen and turned on the dusty old computer that sat there.  It was so old she was impressed it could even turn on.  With a chug sound and a strong whir, the computer started coming to life.

What felt like an eternity later the old computer finally sat at the ready.  Daphne opened her browser and stared at the empty bar for a bit.  Having to resort to manual searching was foreign to Daphne.  How do people know what to put?  She eventually figured she'd ask what she would've asked a spirit if one was near.  She slowly typed 'snuff films' and hit 'Search.'

More chugging and whirring sounded as the computer strained to answer her request.  After a short pause, results started populating the page.  Daphne scanned the listings popping up.  There were news stories, definitions of what snuff films were, blog articles, lots of nothing that would help Daphne figure out how people were actually ordering the snuff films from the *Born Stars*.

On the surface, *Born Stars* was just a video production company.  They could make wedding videos just as easily, so how did they get into this?  Something clawing at Daphne's brain told her there was a bigger operation and she needed to know how it all pieced together.  Starting over at the search bar, Daphne typed 'snuff films and missing girls.'  Again, there was a lot of nothing at first, but then Daphne saw an article that caught her eye.

An investigative journalist had put together an op-ed piece theorizing that the missing girls around Fresno had been part of a large human trafficking ring that was doing a lot more than just abducting and killing girls.  According to this guy, Grace Collins was one of the lucky ones.  And he'd gotten much of his data by going under cover and infiltrating the ring he believed was based right here in the Central Valley of California.

Daphne's heart skipped a beat.  She needed to get a hold of this journalist right away.  Checking the by-line, she saw his name was Robert Stoker.  Desperately hoping he had some type of contact information that was publicly available, Daphne ran a search on his name. If all else failed, she would call The Fresno Bee and just ask for him.  Or just show up.  People had a much harder time blowing you off when you were there in person.  But then again, this guy was obviously a tough cookie to be rolling in and out of a sting operation.

But as the search results slowly started filling the screen, a sense of dread washed over Daphne.  Robert Stoker had died in an accidental fire about a year ago.

It seemed Robert Stoker was closer to the truth than someone wanted him to be.

Daphne called Miguel, her eyes still locked on the screen.  "Change of plans," she told him. "Meet me at 845 Cedar Avenue."

Luckily, she was the one researcher that didn't need her witness to be alive in order to extract the information she needed.

# 19.

It was now just an empty field with overgrown grass and clusters of weeds, bathed in the soft glow of early evening light.  The sky was already beginning to darken, but the sun still danced along the horizon, teasing Daphne with the end of another day.  It seemed a fitting backdrop to the location.  Daphne stood at the site of Robert Stoker's death.  His "accident."  Daphne snorted at the choice of words, knowing full well they were utter bullshit.  She scanned the remnants of the lot looking, seeking, sensing any sign of Robert Stoker's spirit.

There was nothing.

She closed her eyes and held her right hand out in front of herself.  Anytime something traumatic happened, the force of the energy left an imprint on the location. She could tap into that to sense what took place that day in the fire. Suddenly she felt an overwhelming wave of heat, with a force that punched her right in the gut. She stumbled back from the unseen force. An explosion. The heat was intense but she wanted to find out more. She yearned to know *who* was behind this.

Of course, even if she had seen the face of the perpetrator—which she never did—she knew even without using psychic tendencies that whoever was actually behind this would've hired someone to do his dirty work. The person who caused Robert Stoker's death was just a pawn in a wide net of chess pieces.

Just like Rick likely was.

A flash of headlights shook her out of her psychic reading and she turned to watch Miguel pull up and park his car in the street in front of the empty lot.

He hadn't even closed the door yet when he asked, "Is there a particular reason we're meeting here of all places?"   The look on his face said he already suspected some piece of the answer to that question but was offering Daphne the chance to explain.

"I came across an article by an investigative journalist who claimed to have insider knowledge on the Born Stars operation.  He said it was way bigger than those two goofballs and some snuff films, which we already guessed."

"Okay?  Still not connecting the dots on why we're standing in this weed-filled lot."  Miguel was standing close to Daphne and she fought the urge to hold his hand.  She felt so comfortable with him and, oddly, that was making her uncomfortable.

"The journalist, Robert Stoker, died in an 'accidental' fire—"  She used air quotes and a roll of the eyes to tell Miguel she didn't believe a word of the official story.  "—six months after he published that exposé."

"So is his ghost confirming that he died because he knew too much?" Miguel asked.  The very question warmed Daphne's heart.   He wasn't even denying anymore.  He simply trusted her abilities and the truth of the spirit world all around him.

Daphne frowned.  "No, but I think his death does.  I can't sense details, but just being here I know the fire was started by an explosion."

"I can look up the official report.  I don't remember much about it, so it was likely an open and shut case." But as Miguel talked, Daphne saw flashes of a man made of burning embers standing in the back corner of the lot.  There were no facial details, he was charred beyond recognition, but she knew it was Robert Stoker.  He was across the yard from them.  Then in a flash he was in the middle of the yard.  And then, in less than a second, he stood right in front of Miguel.

Miguel had no idea, of course, but the charred remains of the journalist were inches from his face.

"He's here," Daphne said simply, her eyes locked on the burnt and glowing spirit.

Miguel looked around, oblivious to what Daphne could see.  "Where?"

"He's right in front of you.  I think he wants to talk."  At the sound of those words, Robert's burnt face turned sharply toward Daphne. So she decided it was time to get to the point.  "We need to know what you know about the Born Stars."

Miguel just watched the exchange in silence, curious but not afraid of the ghost supposedly standing uncomfortably close.  He'd have never known without Daphne telling him.  Instinctively, he reached out a hand to "feel" the ghost, but it didn't help of course.  He saw and felt nothing.

Robert's charred ghost growled in response.

His anger was emanating from his soul, like a tangible thing.  It made no difference to Daphne.  She'd encountered angry spirits before, and she figured if anyone had a right to be angry it was this guy.

She changed her tactic.  "We know you blame them for your death.  Miguel here is a cop—"  She pointed a thumb at Miguel.  "—and he's trying to put them all behind bars. We want what you want."

The ghost of Robert Stoker stared at Daphne for a long while, his glowing eyes scanning her for truths.  He had been wronged in death—and likely in life—so he was naturally inclined to mistrust people at first.  But Daphne waited patiently.  She knew that look because it was one she often gave, the kind that looks beyond the surface and into your soul.

"I got too close."  Robert's ghost growled out the words.

"I know."  Daphne nodded.

Robert's eyes squinted in anger. "But you don't, or you wouldn't be asking."

"Okay," Daphne answered.  "So help me understand.  I'm on your side, Robert.  I hate what they did to you."

Robert thought about her words for a minute before answering.  "Born Stars is nothing.  Just some lackeys. I don't know if he's the very top, but you need to investigate Ronnie Blackwood.  He owns Bon Apetit.  The restaurant."

"The gray doors," Daphne whispered to herself when something clicked into place for her.  She'd never been to Bon Apetit—wasn't really her scene with its black tie waiters and multiple forks—but she'd driven by enough to know its décor.  It had large, imposing gray double doors on a white and black exterior.  She turned to Miguel.  "The gray doors at the warehouse reminded me of something but I couldn't place it at the time.  Somehow that warehouse is connected to Bon Apetit, the restaurant with the gray doors."

Miguel nodded.  "I believe you.  What else does he say?"

Daphne turned back to Robert.  "Can you tell me the whole story?  How you were able to get in and how they found out?"

Robert's eyes flashed for just a moment before he spoke in his growly voice.  "It's easy to infiltrate that ring if you don't have a soul.  Once I said I wanted in, they pretty much cut me in.  I was a runner.  Swapping 'things' for money for Ronnie."

"Things?" Daphne asked as Miguel watched silently, curious but patient.

"Sometimes illegal films that were made, sometimes girls that were being trafficked, sometimes drugs. Basically anything illegal people will pay for. There's no business model except 'black market'."

"What did you do?"

"I tried to keep my head down so I could break the story, but their operation did make me sick. I guess I got kinda sloppy. I wanted to speed up the breakthrough so I started snooping through financial records. I don't know for sure, but I guess they knew I was a mole."

"Rick and Kyle? What's their deal?"

"They're just henchmen. Lackeys like I was. Selling their souls for money."

"I knew it, those pieces of shit." Daphne's lip curled at the thought of those two morons.

"The thing is, Rick and Kyle are expendable. You capture those two, two more will just take their place. You have to go to the source and I'm certain there is someone above Ronnie Blackwood.  Someone powerful. You'll need to watch your back."

"Noted."  Before Daphne could ask any more questions, Miguel's phone rang.  The instant that happened Robert's ghost disappeared.  Daphne, deflated, watched as Miguel rushed to answer whoever was calling.

After a few nods and "uh-huhs," he hung up the phone and smiled back at Daphne.  "They got 'em.  Rick was picked up at his house and Kyle was trying to run. Caught him in a routine traffic stop."

Daphne shook her head.  "They're just distractions."

"Maybe so, but they're also kidnappers and murderers.  Let's go talk to them at the station."  Miguel nodded toward their parked cars in front of the empty lot.

"Let's?"  Daphne raised an eyebrow questioningly.

"What can I say? I'm beginning to appreciate your

talents."  Miguel opened the passenger door for her. "Ride with me and we can come back for your car later.  I want to hear what Robert the journalist told you."

Daphne looked at Miguel for a moment, taking him in.  What was it about him?  He wasn't anything like the men she was usually attracted to.  He wore a suit and gelled his hair.  She normally found herself drawn to men who were a little bit more on the fringes of society, more like she was.  But this guy was so normal.  So everything she wasn't.  And she was finding that she liked that about him.  Somehow it gave her a balance she hadn't realized until now that she needed.

"All right.  I'll go with you.  Because I know you're not a creepy stalker.  But when you're interrogating witnesses, I get to jump in whenever I want to.  Got it?  If I'm going to help, I'm going to help my way."

He walked over to her and grabbed her hand so gently.  She was annoyed with her heart as its beat began thumping at his close and tender contact.  "Daphne. I've never known anyone like you.  And I have no rational explanation for any of this.  But watching you work?  I'm starting to really like it. You can help your way anytime you want."  He gestured toward the car.  "Come on."

He placed his hand at the small of her back and guided her gently toward the passenger seat.  No one had ever shown her such tenderness.  Not in a romantic way, at least.  The wall that she had spent years building up was slowly starting to erode with Miguel, and she was happy and terrified at the same time.

When they were in the car, she turned to him. "I'm really bad with people skills.  And even worse with relationships.   But you know what I'm good at?  Disarming people who think they know everything.  Let's go put these assholes away and break up the Born Stars crime syndicate."

Miguel smiled at her as he turned the engine. "Which is exactly why we make such a great team."

His smile made her feel like a teenager, which was annoying her, so she did as she always did when she felt vulnerable: she changed the subject.  "Robert's ghost said to look into Ronnie Blackwood who owns the Bon Appetit restaurant.  But he also said that even Ronnie wasn't the top."

Miguel nodded, intensely listening to everything she had to say.  His headlights lit up the street before them as he continued driving downtown. "Okay.  There are lots of players.  Got it."

Daphne shifted in her seat.  Was she nervous for Miguel's safety?  She hated caring this much for living people.  "They killed Robert when he got too close.  You have to be careful.  They'd sacrifice a cop in an instant if it meant protecting their crime spree."

Miguel grabbed her hand and squeezed.  She didn't pull away.  He knew where she was coming from because he'd felt the same need to protect her safety when they were at the warehouse to get Ellie.  But if he really thought about it, they were probably both used to evil in this world.  A dark soul is a dark soul, whether living or dead.

"Trust me when I say, there's always someone

out there who wants me dead. I'm trained for this so you don't have to worry."

Daphne stared at their intertwined fingers and fought the urge to deny that she was worried. Denial was her instinct, but she knew they both knew it was nonsense. So she focused on the case.

If she focused on how much she enjoyed him holding her hand or on the fact she cared if he was targeted by the Born Stars Crime Syndicate, all the feelings she'd spent years bottling up would explode. The hurt at not being accepted. The pain at rejection by her own family. The loneliness of being an outcast. All there buried in a heap along with truly and deeply caring for another human being.

"My guess is the real mastermind here isn't the idiot that Rick and Kyle are," Daphne snorted.

Miguel smiled, seeing through her diversion. He didn't mind. He rarely let his guard down either. "No doubt." He paused for a moment, thinking. "Remember how you told me visions just sometimes popped into your head?  Well, I guess it's kinda like that.  We get a piece of the puzzle, sometimes one at a time, sometimes in a big heap like the boat today, but we just keep piling up the pieces until they form the full picture."

Daphne understood, so she nodded.

Miguel continued.  "Rick and Kyle, the lower end of the gene pool, are just pieces that help us pull everything together."

Daphne pulled her hand out of Miguel's just so she could ball her hand in a fist.  "Perfect. Then let's go squeeze these guys for all they've got.  And I'll know if they lie."

Miguel pushed on the accelerator and they raced to the interrogation.

# 20.

The sun had finally set and the warm Fresno air had finally gotten refreshingly cooler.  It wasn't cool, by any means, but a comfortable night air.  Most people were settling in for the night.  Miguel would just be starting his.

He reached back and grabbed Daphne's hand as they approached the glass front doors of the downtown Fresno precinct.  It had happened so naturally, he hadn't even thought about it until they were about to enter the building. She hadn't pulled away, he noticed.

There was something so weird, and at the same time comforting, to know they were linked in ways that couldn't be understood logically.

The whole front of the building was glass, so people were bound to notice he was holding the witness's hand.  He decided he didn't care.  He couldn't explain it to anyone, but the policing world was like a private club—you may not like everyone, but you were all in this together.  By morning, everyone would know something was going on between him and Daphne, if they didn't already.

He had texted Gina to let her know they were on their way and she dutifully waited in the lobby.  She glanced at Miguel's hand in Daphne's but said nothing. Didn't even give him a side eye, so he wasn't sure how to take it.  Likely, she simply didn't care. They had Belton and Kyle by the balls and that was way more important to Gina right now.

"Belton's in room 1. Kyle is in 3."  Gina gestured down the hall with a nod of her head.  Daphne remembered the drab hallway from her first visit here. "So how do you want to do this?"  She looked between Miguel and Daphne, but he knew immediately what she was asking.  They had never interrogated a witness as a threesome before.

Miguel opened his mouth to respond, but Daphne beat him to it.  "Just use me as your lie detector test.  I won't talk unless I need to.  I'll just stand in the corner and give a signal when they're lying."

Gina nodded.  "I like that. What signal?"

"A whistle?"

"A clap?"

"How about I clear my throat?"

Miguel looked at the two women.  "Does my opinion matter here?"

"What's your idea?" Gina asked honestly.

Miguel frowned.  He hadn't really had one, he just suddenly felt like the third wheel had gone from Daphne to him in an instant.  "I like the clearing-the-throat signal."

"Belton or KKK?"  Gina was asking who he wanted to start with.

"As much as I hate Kevin K. Kyle Consulting, I

think we start with Rick.  Daphne's stumbled upon some new intel that confirms your instinct that this is bigger than these two.  If we can get some leverage from Rick, we can use it against KKK."

"Stumbled across some intel?  Do I want to know?"  Gina raised an eyebrow.

"I talked to the spirit of a reporter who got a little too close and paid for it with his life," Daphne explained.

"So we have two ghosts as witnesses now?" Gina asked. There was no judgment, just a desire to understand what she'd missed.

"There's always going to be more ghosts," Daphne sighed.

Gina mulled something over in her mind but said nothing.

"Rick it is, then.  Let's go."  Gina gestured again and then started walking.

Miguel dropped Daphne's hand—not because he wanted to but because he didn't want to give the suspects any ammunition against him.  If they knew how he felt about her, it would give them leverage.  Daphne understood completely, even without her intuition.  She wasn't always in Cayman's investigations back in Los Angeles, but she knew enough from when she was that being guarded was the key.

Gina entered the room first.

Rick Bersin-slash-Belton was nothing like the photo on the Born Stars website.  Daphne had expected that, but Gina had been a little surprised.  She'd had an image in her head and it was not the man who sat before her.

First of all, there was fear in his eyes.  He knew his goose was cooked.  Good.  At least he had some common sense.  Secondly, this man was anything but clean cut.  Either he'd been letting himself go for the past two weeks, or this unkempt stoner look was his ploy to attract teenage girls.  Brown curly hair, like Mrs. Collins had first described, but muscular?  Not anymore.  Gina had a hard time believing Grace Collins would ever get in a car with this guy, believing he would make her a star.

The only thing he looked like was a drug dealer.

"Let's talk about your Born Stars business," Gina stated flatly as she pulled out a chair across from the suspect and sat down.  Daphne was impressed with her professionalism, tough and solid.

Rick startled a bit, clearly expecting them to ask about something else.  That got Daphne's senses on high alert as she watched him shift uncomfortably in his chair.  This guy clearly wasn't used to being brought in by the law.  He had zero poker face.

"I make movies," he said with his chin up, trying too late to fake bravado.

"Can you elaborate? What kind of movies? Who do you make them for?"

"Corporate videos for local businesses."

"We're going to need a list of your clients," Miguel said, jumping in, choosing to stand next to where Gina was sitting.  Daphne stood in the corner, silently watching.  She knew he was full of baloney even with his first answer, but she figured she'd save her signal for when he told a lie Gina and Miguel couldn't see right through.

"Of course," Rick answered. Another flash of fear crossed his eyes and he swallowed hard. The realization hit Daphne hard—he wasn't scared because of the interrogation. He knew this meant he was dead. Whoever was masterminding everything would just sacrifice this lamb without a care in the world.

And Rick knew it.

What a sad state of the world when there were so many people in line to do your dirty work that you could just kill your henchmen without a second thought.

"We found the jewelry on your boat, Rick. We can tie you to multiple kidnappings and murders," Miguel stated.

A bead of sweat broke out on Rick's upper lip, but he said nothing. He couldn't. Anything he said would sign his death warrant. It was likely too late already.

"If you take us to the bodies of the victims, we can see what we can do about a plea deal," Gina said.

Rick just shifted in his seat again.  There was nothing he could say.

As Daphne watched Rick, the wheels turning in his head of how to get out of this mess he found himself in, a gust of wind at her side alerted her to the fact that Grace had shown up.

"Forget this guy," Grace said.  "Ronnie has my mom."

"What?" Daphne responded in shock before she could stop herself.  All eyes in the interrogation room turned her way.

"You go after Ronnie and I'll handle Rick.  This will be fun."  Grace smiled.  There was only so much she could do, but scaring the man who murdered her would give Grace some sense of satisfaction.

Suddenly and without warning, Rick flew back against the wall behind him, his chair legs screeching on the floor beneath him.  He hit his head hard.

"What the hell, man?" Rick asked Miguel, but Miguel turned immediately to Daphne.

Daphne answered his unvoiced question with, "Grace's here.  And she'd like a turn interrogating the witness."

Suddenly the metal table flipped on its side, clanking as it hit the floor.

"Daphne?" Miguel asked.  Gina just stood up and backed away.  She was too shocked to say anything.

Grace's voice echoed in the interrogation room as if it were coming from an overhead speaker.  "You're dead, Rick.  And when the end comes for you, I'll be there to watch as you're dragged to Hell."

Rick twisted in his seat, still rubbing his head, not able to believe what was happening around him.

"Daphne, why do we hear her?" Miguel asked, a look of disbelief painted clearly across his face.

Daphne simply shrugged, the only person in the room not totally bewildered.  "Anger is a powerful emotion. It feeds energy. So does fear." She gestured to Rick.  "She's angry.  He's afraid.  And it's fueling Grace's spirit."

Rick was forcibly lifted by an unseen hand and dragged up against the wall, his feet dangling beneath him.  Grace's voice echoed again, "Ronnie Blackwood. Where is he?"

"I don't know."  Rick shook his head, his voice trembling.  The man who trafficked, raped and murdered girls on film for money was cowering before Grace's ghost.  Daphne couldn't help the small smile that crept across her lips at the irony.

Daphne could see Grace squeeze Rick's neck, but Miguel and Gina only knew something was happening by the choking sounds coming from the man in their custody. They stared, frozen in awe at the sight of their witness dangling before them with the force of an unseen entity.

"We both know you're already dead.  Don't die with my mother's blood on your hands too," Grace's voice echoed.

"Okay," Rick barely managed to say.  At that, he slowly began lowering down the wall, air resuming into his lungs.  He rubbed his throat and coughed before saying, "He's at the compound."

"Compound?" Miguel asked, still confused but trying to catch up quickly.  He'd need to ask Daphne a few questions on his own.

"Ronnie is the glue between the boss and us guys who do the actual work," Rick said, doubled over, still rubbing his throat.  "He meets with the boss at the compound every week."

"How many guys who 'do the actual work' are there?" Gina jumped in.

Rick shook his head. "I don't know."

"What would Ronnie and this boss guy want with Mrs. Collins?" Miguel asked.

"I don't know."

"He's telling the truth," Daphne blurted from where she'd been calmly watching the whole scene play out.  "The ring has all these various limbs so they can be easily removed and avoid law enforcement connecting it to the head.  He's in the dark on purpose."

"So I take it you don't know where the compound is?" Miguel asked Rick.

Rick shook his head.

Grace spoke to Daphne, this time she was calmer and her voice wasn't echoing throughout the room.  "He doesn't, but I think I do."

"We can trace Ronnie Blackwood's phone, but we'll need time to get the warrant," Gina said.

"There's no time," Grace said.  "You've gotta go. I can lead you."

"I don't need a warrant."  Daphne pushed off the wall and started walking toward the door.  "And Grace can tell me where to go."

"Daphne."  Miguel was unable to hide his concern for her safety.

"Don't worry.  I won't do anything stupid." Daphne fanned his concern away with her hand.

"You're not going by yourself."

"You can both go.  There's a possible hostage situation," Gina said, her lips tight.  "I got these two lackeys."

Miguel nodded at Gina and started to leave.

From where he stood up against the wall, still shaken from his paranormal encounter, Rick spoke plainly, with no dramatic flair or threat to his tone. He simply stated facts. "If you find the compound, you're both dead."

# 21.

"How do you know where the compound is?" Daphne asked Grace once they were all in Miguel's car.

"When they took my mom, I followed," Grace explained to only Daphne. Without her anger and fervor at the man who murdered her, she wasn't able to make her voice echo throughout the car so Miguel could hear it too. "I had no idea it was their compound, just that it was another strange place where they hide people. Then I went to you."

Grace instructed Daphne where to go and she interpreted for Miguel. It wasn't far from where they had just been at the Fresno Police Department downtown headquarters. A few twists and turns and they were in front of an older home that looked like it was built in the early 1900's. It had a Victorian flair to it, two-story with a large front porch and high arches on the second floor. While it wasn't very far from office buildings and homes that had been converted into doctor's offices and such, it appeared to be a normal residence.

"Are we sure?" Miguel asked Daphne. Daphne simply shrugged in response.

"They took my mom around back," Grace explained. "Give me a minute."

Grace disappeared from the car and Daphne told Miguel that she had gone inside, presumably to locate her mother.

"So what made you adamant that you come here?" Miguel asked Daphne. "We could've handled it. You seem to love to put yourself in danger." He was worried about her, but he also wanted to understand her. It's a far cry from talking to ghosts to putting yourself in mortal danger.

"If I can save someone, I want to save them. I

*need* to save them," Daphne explained.

"But you help ghosts normally."

Daphne shifted in her seat.  "So what's your question?"  She knew what he was asking her, but she wanted to hear him voice it.

"You could've told me everything you know from the comfort of your own home over the phone.  Grace Collins' friend is saved and her murderer captured.  But you had to come here to the compound?  Why?  Why face a criminal ring that could endanger your life?"

She could see the wrinkle of Miguel's brow as he tried to understand her.  The care on his face knocked a few more of the bricks in her façade loose.  She'd never had to explain herself before and wasn't even sure if she could.  A few more fissures and her walls might come crumbling down.  After a lifetime of talking to ghosts and chasing murderers, this was the one thing that truly terrified her.

But there was something about this guy.

Daphne sighed.  "There's a spirit of a little girl.

Maddy.  Madison Laurens.  She's a cold case in Los Angeles.  She was tortured and killed over twenty years ago.  Cayman and I never found her body or her killer.  And she haunts me to this day."  An image of Maddy pleading for Daphne's help flashed into her mind.  "This may come as a shock to you, but this gift of mine never won me any Miss Congeniality awards.  Mostly it lost me friends and loved ones.  But if I can use what I can do to help one person, I'm going to do it.  I don't know what else to do with myself otherwise."  Daphne sat back and leaned her head against the headrest.  "I can't silence the spirits any other way."

Miguel smiled gently, but there was a sadness in his eyes.  "We're the same in a lot of ways, you know that?  It may not be ghosts that haunt me, but I understand needing to do everything you can for a victim. I have cases that I can't let go of either."

Miguel looked out over his shoulder, peering at the house Grace's ghost had taken them to.  Daphne was here for Grace and Miguel was here for Mrs. Collins. In the end, it didn't really matter what brought them here. Neither was going to leave this place without doing what they had to.

Miguel thought it was odd that the whole front of the house was dark.  No streetlights.  No porch light.  No interior lamps lit.

Miguel shook his head.  "This just doesn't seem right."

Daphne held her hand up and closed her eyes, sensing the story of this older home.  After a moment she told Miguel, "I don't know if this is what they call their compound or not, but it's definitely something.  Lots of people are held here against their will."

"Like human trafficking?"

"Possibly.  I sense a lot of fear.  Not just from the hostages, but the workers too.  Whoever tells them what to do scares them."

"I'm not surprised.  If Rick is certain he's dead, then clearly whoever is behind all this has no qualms about killing people."

"Rick *is* as good as dead.  No way they'll leave him and Kyle as loose ends.  But this is different.  This is someone commanding and powerful.  I'm sensing a politician or something along those lines.  Someone who thinks he's above the law."

"Do you see a face?"

Daphne shook her head, but before she could say more, Miguel jumped in his seat at a loud bang on his window.

"It's Grace," Daphne said, explaining the noise. "She found her mom.  Let's go."

Daphne climbed out of the car without hesitation.  Miguel was surprised she was so fearless.  He knew she'd gotten desensitized to the supernatural, but these were real criminals with real weapons.

"Stay behind me," he instructed Daphne, although he half-expected her to argue.  She didn't.  She knew he was saying it to protect her and she was finding that she liked that.  Normally, someone coddling her annoyed her, but that was different.  Those people had always wanted to hold her back or were frightened and confused by her.  Miguel respected her, and that made all the difference.

Grace crooked her finger at Daphne, silently instructing them to follow her.

"Go around back," Daphne whispered to Miguel, and he nodded in return.  When they made it to the side of the house, he drew his weapon and held it at the ready.  He had no idea what they might stumble upon, although his goal was to get Mrs. Collins and get out as undetected as possible.

As they rounded the corner to the back of the house, Daphne closely behind Miguel, he was surprised to see no one guarding the back door.  He exhaled the relief before continuing forward.  His steps were careful and controlled.  Slowly moving forward, toe heel, toe heel.  He was painfully aware that a single misstep could cost him and Daphne both their lives.

From the back door, Daphne watched Grace glide through the door as easily as if it had been open.  Not wanting to risk making a sound, Daphne simply pointed to let Miguel know where Grace had gone.  He nodded in return.  It's what he'd expected all along.  Unless there had been a basement entrance, that back door is where they were headed.

Fortunately, there were no lights in the backyard either.  They were able to move carefully forward in the blanket of darkness.  Only the sound of a cricket singing somewhere in the night provided any sign of life.

He paused for only a moment when they reached the door before grabbing the handle and turning the doorknob.  The guard that wasn't posted on the outside could be just inside the door.  The door handle turned easily—It wasn't locked.  When it had reached its full turn, Miguel pulled quickly and purposefully to open it, standing in a shooting stance with his gun stretched before him.

No one was there.

While he peered into the darkness of the old home, Daphne squeezed around him, using her psychic abilities to know there was no one in the room they were about to enter. As she passed him, she leaned in to whisper, "The guards are in the bedroom where the victims are, but that was super sexy."

Grace stood in the center of the room they had just entered. It looked like a classic sitting room of some sort. A bookshelf lined the back wall and a couch with matching settee sat in the middle of the room. It was all very posh. Daphne realized she knew no one who actually used a settee. And she wasn't sure she would want to.

As they crept forward as silently as they could, Grace gestured again. The darkness of the room gave her an eerie glow, allowing her to look more like a classic ghost than she ever had so far. She glided through a glass door and turned left down a dark hallway.

Daphne turned back to Miguel and pointed to inform him of the direction they were heading, and they both moved forward slowly and quietly.

But the silence of the house wouldn't last long.

Just as they entered the hallway, the sound of arguing came barreling down the stairs.  It was two men, and they were shouting at one another, clearly at odds on whatever topic they had been discussing.

Naturally, Miguel turned toward the sound of the men and Daphne grabbed his arm to stop him.  She shook her head and again pointed down the dark hallway in the direction Grace had gone.  They were here to save Mrs. Collins and she was in the opposite direction from the stairs.

Miguel leaned in to Daphne's ear so he could speak as softly as possible.  "I know that voice."  He headed over to the stairs and Daphne let him go.  He had his work to do and she had hers.  After all, Mrs. Collins and Grace were just one piece of this case for Miguel.  And Daphne wasn't leaving without Mrs. Collins being freed.  She supposed it was time to divide and conquer.

And hadn't Daphne originally planned to come here alone all along anyway?

Miguel felt really exposed climbing the stairs.  He

kept his gun at the ready, but since he'd become a detective, the actual confrontations with perpetrators were increasingly rare. And since he'd deviated from the game plan of finding Mrs. Collins, he now greatly regretted that he hadn't called in a team. But that voice... He had to know if someone he knew were connected with this whole thing.

The shouting got louder, suddenly followed by a loud crash. The fighting was intensifying. Miguel was going on instinct now—he had no plan of what he would do when he stumbled across the murdering thugs who were running the black-market ring. He didn't even know how many people total were in that room.

Miguel hugged the wall as he approached the room with the arguing and the familiar voice. The door was open and he was able to get enough of a peek inside to see that he'd been right about the voice he recognized.

Judge Bustamante.

The judge who'd been a pain in his ass his whole career was in there fighting with a bald man in his early forties.  Ronnie Blackwood, maybe?

And something they were working on had gone horribly awry.  At first, Miguel thought maybe they were upset about Rick Belton getting arrested.  But after listening to them, it sounded bigger than that.

"You stupid asshole!  You've been too sloppy!" The judge, red-faced, screamed at the bald man, his big round face contorted with anger.

"Sloppy?  I put everything on that boat just as you instructed me to.  If there's sloppiness here, it's on you!"

"You made this mess, now you need to clean it up.  I need the merchandise moved NOW."  Judge Bustamante struck the desk with his fat fist.

"Maybe you should try getting your hands a little dirty yourself.  You sit in your ivory tower with your pristine cuticles while I take all the risks."  The bald man was getting in the judge's face.  Miguel leaned in, curious to know what their big concern at the moment was.  Was it just the local P.D. they were worried about?  Or had the

Born Stars boat gotten them in hot water with the Feds? Or another rival gang?

"I want everything out of this house tonight," the judge stated.  His voice was still laced with anger, but it was controlled and forceful.  He was a man who was used to getting his way.

"Nothing traces back to you.  Have a little more faith in me than that."  The bald man had calmed down a bit.  Emotions and tensions were still high in the room, but they were no longer at each other's throats.  They now had the air of people who had to get a job done, no matter the cost.  "I've served you faithfully for decades. We've built everything together. No stupid fucking drug lord is going to come along and unravel everything now."

So, it was a rival ring.

"Ronnie, you have to understand.  These guys? They use the same tricks I do.  They'll plant evidence here just to get us out of the way."

"Then forget about moving the drugs.  We have lots of other customers.  No need to create an enemy we don't need."

The judge was angry again, his wide chest heaving. "This is my territory! Just clear the house out today and lay low. Why are you so thick-headed?"

There was silence for a moment and then footsteps making their way to the doorway toward the eavesdropper they'd been unaware of.

Miguel hugged the wall, trying to plan his escape. There was no place to run to without being seen.

And it was too late.

Ronnie Blackwood, the bald man fighting with Judge Bustamante, stood before him. And their eyes locked.

Before Miguel could instruct the criminal before him to freeze, Ronnie lunged at him and Miguel moved to defend himself. Ronnie grabbed at his arms, too close for Miguel to aim the gun that was still in his hand. Miguel knocked his arms loose and Ronnie swung for his face. He tried to move out of the way, but Ronnie's fist connected with Miguel's jaw, sending a shockwave through his bones.  On instinct Miguel swung back.  It wasn't a solid hit, but it knocked Ronnie backward, stumbling in the second-floor hallway.

This gave Miguel time to aim.  He raised his gun, but Ronnie wasn't too stunned to react.  Ronnie ran at him, full force, tackling him to the ground.

Judge Bustamante watched the whole thing and did nothing.  Ronnie was right—he didn't like to get his hands dirty.

# 22.

Daphne moved quietly down the hall, going as slowly as she could toward the room where Grace was leading her. She knew by now where they were headed. There was only one door closed with light seeping through the bottom. The rest of the house was dark.

What she didn't know was what she would find when she opened the door.

Daphne wasn't afraid of dying. Not even close. She'd met enough dead people in her life that the fear of the unknown factor that so many people had just wasn't a thing for her. But she was afraid of being captured and sold into a sex ring or something.

And she was afraid of losing Miguel. Dammit.

She had to admit it. Now that she'd found him, she had something to lose. She could run from Duane. She could run from Cayman. She could hide behind ghosts and cold cases. But she couldn't run and hide from her feelings for Miguel.

She had something to live for and it changed *everything*.

Her heart started pounding in anticipation as she approached the door. She had to use everything at her advantage and she did have one thing they didn't—a vengeful ghost.

"How many are there?" she whispered in the dark hallway to Grace.

"Two guards. Eight women," Grace answered, her voice loud and clear to Daphne.

Daphne looked around for something—anything—that would help her defend herself against two presumably armed guards.

Grace pointed to a room to the right. There were no lights on, but as she entered it seemed like some old-fashioned library. This entire house was like walking into a time machine. No one had rooms like this anymore, did they? But at the far wall she saw what Grace was pointing to.

There was a large fireplace that looked like it hadn't been used in decades. But at its base sat a fire poker stand. And a wrought iron fire poker would do just fine. She grabbed it and crept back to the door with the light.

She rested her hand on the door handle and took in a large breath. Momentarily she thought about Miguel's question. Why *was* she putting herself in danger right now? As stupid as she felt, she knew the answer. There were women on the other side who'd been victimized. And she wasn't leaving without them.

With a nod to Grace, Daphne opened the door and surprise-attacked the armed guard who was sitting just inside the door. And thank goodness for Grace. She materialized before the other guard long enough to stun him into inaction, just before she shoved him across the room, the rifle that had been across his lap skidding to the floor and sliding out of his reach.

Meanwhile, the women in the room were screaming as Daphne struck the guard she was fighting hard across the face, sending spit, blood and a tooth flying out of his mouth and onto the floor. She struck his arms next so that his gun was also freed, thudding to the floor.

The women in the room were tied up, so they couldn't go far, but instinctively they pulled back from the violence happening around them and the ghost appearing before them.

Moving quickly to subdue her guard, Daphne struck him again, this time in the back, so he fell to the floor and she had to look quickly for something to tie this guy up. Both guards must've been stunned, because they weren't fighting back nearly like Daphne had expected.

The surprise ghost-attack had been everything she'd hoped for and more.

Out of the corner of her eye, Daphne noticed

Grace pushing down on the guard she was fighting.  He stared wide-eyed, unable to fully process that a ghost was kicking his ass.  But she didn't stop to enjoy that.  The large dresser in the corner of the room was calling to her.

She opened the first drawer and a bunch of papers came flying out.  The second drawer had various articles of women's clothing.  But the third drawer had what she'd been looking for and sensed was in the room.  There were bandanas, strips of cotton cloth and chloroform, a hunting knife and rope.  Bingo.  She'd found the kidnapper's treasure trove.  Grabbing the rope, she made a mental note to ponder later about the twistedness of a drawer like that.

When she turned around to tie up the guard she'd been fighting, she saw him stumbling toward her, his arm raised.  He looked crazed, drunk even.  But it didn't stop him from bringing his hand down across her face.  Hard.  Daphne stumbled back into the dresser, the pain from her face and now her back shooting up her spine and dizzying her with the intensity.  She knew she needed to recover quickly, but that was easier said than done.

The guard came at her again, clutching her throat and squeezing with one hand.  Daphne stared into his crazed eyes and in them saw reflections of all the women and young girls that had passed by this asshole.  He had ensured the fates of many an innocent girl, and it made her sick.  The image of each and every girl, and all their emotions of fear, rage, depression, came flashing into Daphne's mind with rapid fire.  She wanted to kick him in the balls in retaliation once for every girl, but she was too focused on the hand at her throat.  She struggled to get free so she could breathe.

Just as the dark spots were beginning to appear at the edges of her vision, the guard at her throat was picked up and slammed against the far wall.  As she rubbed her throat, she saw an angry Grace holding the other guard high in the air, feet dangling.  Dizzy from the lack of oxygen, she knew she had to act now or never.  There were too many faces in this room that needed her to succeed.

Using the dresser she had hit as a crutch, she pushed herself along toward the guard that had been choking her.  She grabbed his arms and yanked them behind his back.  He barely resisted because his mind was so focused on processing how he'd been thrown by a ghost.  She tied him as tight as she could, relishing every yank and twist.  And when she was done and he was safely secured where he couldn't hurt anyone anymore, Daphne pulled her foot back and plunged it straight into his crotch.

"That's for every girl you ever hurt," Daphne spit in his face.

"Daphne.  Hurry."  Grace called her over to the second guard, the one Grace had pretty much incapacitated since the moment they walked into the room.  Daphne tied him up just like the other guy as Grace sat with her mother, her arm gently around her shoulders.  When the second guard was also hogtied, Daphne pulled out her cell phone and called Detective

Gina Malone.

She had just finished telling Gina what she'd stumbled upon when a loud bang echoed throughout the old Victorian home. The blood drained from Daphne's face.

Daphne spoke into the phone to Gina.  "Oh, shit. Miguel followed a familiar voice upstairs.  And I think I just heard a gunshot."

# 23.

Judge Bustamante wiped the gun clean and placed it back into the top drawer.  He had worked so hard to keep himself far enough away from the crime syndicate as to never get caught.  He wasn't going to take the fall for it all now.

Stepping over the bleeding bodies of Ronnie Blackwood, his longtime partner, and Miguel Alvarez, the detective he'd always hated for his holier-than-thou approach to justice, the judge waltzed calmly toward the stairs.

Of course, he had no idea Daphne and the ghost of one of his victims were downstairs and had heard everything.

He'd been more worried about the drug lord who was encroaching onto his turf. His arrogance was blinding him to reality. After all, he hadn't been caught for all these years, right? So who could pin him down now? The main man who could connect him to everything was now lying in a pool of his own blood—and dead men tell no tales. And who wouldn't accept anything he stated publicly? Judge Bustamante was a well-respected judge in this community.

And he'd worked hard to become so.

It wasn't like he was from a wealthy family of means. He'd had to pull himself out of poverty, going to college on the G.I. bill. And as he came to prominence in the justice community, he realized there was a lot of money to be made on the back side of the law. And it was easy to make deals with criminals when you were their judge. A little "time off for good behavior" here and there and then they owed you.

That's how he'd first met Ronnie.

Ronnie Blackwood had been a small-time hustler

when he'd first crossed paths with the heavyset judge. But Judge Bustamante had seen his potential and he'd absolutely turned out to be right.  Jail time turned into community service and then Ronnie owed him.  And Judge Bustamante had turned him from a two-bit crook to a crime lord.  Ronnie had only wanted to make his restaurant a success—all his petty crimes had been in the name of helping his business thrive—but it had turned out to be the perfect front for everything.

No one suspected a local, prominent restaurateur any more than they suspected a well-respected judge.

And luring "business partners" had been easy. They felt invincible with Ronnie backing them and the promise of easy money never hurt anyone.  Little did they know that they were just fishing line—easily cut when the going got rough.  Thrown to the lions to take the fall.

Just like Rick Belton.  He'd been getting too big for his britches anyway.  Leaving a trail of bodies everywhere he went.  Someone was bound to notice at some point.  The judge had always preferred his victims alive.  It's harder to profit from someone who's dead.  No matter.  Now that Rick was behind bars, he had served his purpose.  They'd just have to have someone in the prison system dispose of him before he talked too broadly.

Guys like Rick always had big mouths when they were scared.

Judge Bustamante continued walking casually down the stairs when he heard footsteps coming toward him from down the hall.  He stopped, expecting to see one of his guards with perhaps an update on the situation with their latest batch of girls.  But instead, he blinked away his confusion when he saw a young woman with short, spiky blonde hair and a long skirt she wore with thick boots.

This weirdo was far from the type of woman they typically abducted.  The judge liked them wholesome, clean, all-American.  This woman looked like a modern-day Manson follower.

"What are you doing here?" the judge demanded of the woman now bounding up the stairs.

"You better pray he's alive, asshole."  The woman stared him down, which angered him.  Did she not know who he was?  But then again, good if she didn't.  He could still sneak out of here and claim ignorance.  When she was just a few steps below the judge, she turned back over her shoulder and spoke to the thin air.  "Don't let him leave, Grace."

Grace?  The dead girl?

In his anger, he let his emotions slip and he grabbed the blonde girl as she stood on the stair next to him.  "You go up there and you're as good as dead."

She stared deep into his eyes in a way that unsettled him.  And then she said, "You really believe you're invincible.  But we've got you by your balls now, *Judge*."  Daphne shook free and then continued hurrying up the stairs, her number one priority to find out who'd just been shot.

Something about the way she'd looked at him and spoke to him made him freeze for a moment.  But only a moment.  He knew he had to get out of there now or go back and murder the freaky blonde. Deciding it was best to live to fight another day, he continued his coward's escape. There was no evidence that suggested he was tied to anything. Plausible deniability. It would just be one weirdo's word against his.

And that was a gamble he felt he could easily take.

But at the bottom of the stairs, he saw the dead girl. He recognized her from the snuff film and then the evening news. This was her, standing before him. And yet, he'd watched her die on that film.

And furthermore, she looked dead now. Grace had chosen to appear as she'd first shown up for Daphne: black and blue with twigs in her tangled hair.

She stood at the bottom of the stairs, translucent in the dark hallway, but solid enough that he could see her throat slashed from side to side. Her skin was a putrid green, the flesh beginning to rot and fall apart from time spent in the water.

Not sure he'd be able to hear her anyway, she

chose to gesture instead of speak.  She wagged a finger back and forth to let him know he wasn't leaving.  He stared at her wide-eyed, but he continued to walk forward, most likely not trusting what his eyes were seeing.

But there was no way Grace was going to let this creep waltz out the back door.

He had stolen youths.  Kidnapped girls.  Sold, raped, murdered many a woman without a second thought.  And he still thought he was going to get away with it.  And Grace's soul couldn't rest until this fat man's belief system came crumbling down and he ended up in prison, getting back everything he gave tenfold.

She grabbed him and shoved him up against the wall.  He was easily two hundred and sixty pounds but he felt weightless in her grip.  He didn't even try to fight her.  She knew she could keep him pinned until Gina arrived with police back-up, but just for good measure she took her ghostly nails and scratched him across the face.  He yelled in fear and confusion and Grace smiled wickedly to herself.

Unfortunately, Daphne couldn't stay to enjoy the judge's come-uppance. She had to make sure Miguel wasn't the one who'd been shot. It was her singular focus.

As she rounded the corner at the top of the stairs, the first thing she noticed was the enormous pool of blood. It struck her in an instant that she *knew* Miguel had been hit. But so had the other guy.

They both sat there bleeding, the bald man reaching out to her for help, his bloody hand stretched toward her. She couldn't worry about him. She ran to Miguel, kneeling in the blood-drenched carpet, her skirt becoming warm and sticky from it. His whole chest was bloody, but she found the wound easily in his left shoulder. Without stopping to think, she ripped the bottom of her skirt and created a homemade bandage, wrapping it tightly around his shoulder.

"I'm okay," Miguel whispered to Daphne. "Judge Bustamante. Don't let him get away."

"Like hell you are," she responded sternly, worry and fear making her tone sharp. "And don't worry. Grace's got the Judge. He's not going anywhere."

"Grace," Miguel whispered and then smiled softly, closing his eyes.

"Gina's on her way. She'll help me with the women downstairs. Mrs. Collins is there too." Daphne stroked his forehead, speaking more calmly now. His color was getting too pale. She didn't like it. Her heart was pounding in her chest and it wasn't from fighting the guards and it wasn't from running up the stairs. She'd finally found someone she truly connected with, someone she actually trusted with her heart, and she was afraid he'd soon be visiting her in spirit like so many of her "friends."

And, regardless of her comfort with ghosts, she didn't want that at all. She sat next to him and pulled him close to her chest, covering herself in his blood in the process.

The bald man still reached out to her, croaking

out the words, "Help me."

She curled her lip. "Eat shit, douchebag."

"Your face," Miguel said softly to Daphne. "I'm sorry I didn't protect you."

"Shh." Daphne stroked his hair. The hair that was always too perfect. She never cared if her hair looked good or if it looked like she'd stuck her finger in the light socket. Something about the fact he was so opposite from her made her feel more complete. Like a yin and yang symbol coming together. "I had Grace. And we got those guys good. Everyone's a big tough guy until a ghost throws them against the wall. Then shit gets real."

Miguel laughed softly before he whispered so softly, "I love you."

Daphne stilled. No one had said that to her. Ever.

But she didn't have time to process it or say anything in response. The wail of sirens was getting loud enough for her to know that help had arrived.

Making sure Miguel was resting carefully propped against the wall, Daphne said, "Gina's here." And she stood up running back to the top of the stairs. "Let him drop the second the cops walk through the door. Hard."

Grace smiled back at Daphne and when they heard the door open, she heaved Judge Bustamante across the hallway, letting his large body land with a heavy thud.

As Gina entered with six uniforms at her side, Daphne rushed to give as much explanation as she could. Pointing down the hall she yelled, "The women are in the room at the end of the hallway." Then she pointed at the fat man in a heap on the floor. "He's behind everything." And then she sobered a bit, looking straight at Gina. "Miguel's been shot."

"We need a medic," Gina shouted behind her and then ran up the stairs to her partner. When she reached Daphne, she looked her up and down. Her bloodstained clothes and skin. Her black eye from her fight with the guard. "I thought the plan was just to help Mrs. Collins."

Daphne shrugged.  "No big deal.  We just saved eight women and stopped the whole crime ring."

Gina smiled. It was a heavy smile that bore all the weight of the bust going on around them, but it was filled with gratitude too.  "Thanks, Daphne.  You did good."

# 24.

Miguel sat up in his stretcher as they wheeled him toward the ambulance, his shoulder bandaged and his arm in a sling from the onsite treatment by the paramedics. He and Ronnie were both on their way to the hospital, looking like their prognosis was good.

"Did they get him?" Miguel asked Daphne. She knew what he meant. He was talking about Judge Bustamante.

"Yeah. Grace wouldn't let him leave. She helped stop her murderer and save her mom, just like she promised she would."

"Why?" Miguel's head was still leading a struggle for him to keep up. He was weak with blood loss. And likely pain.  "Why do some ghosts stay and help, and others cross over right after they're killed?"

"Some people embrace their death and the afterlife.  Some people are too angry and upset at their death to be at peace.  Or worried.  I think Grace might have been worried about Ellie.  Of course, it turned out that her worries were right."  Daphne gently stroked Miguel's arm as they went to lift him into the ambulance. "Wait."  The paramedics paused and Daphne leaned in to give him a quick kiss.  She couldn't believe the relief she felt at seeing him alive.  And knowing he loved her.  They lifted him into the ambulance and she watched it drive away.

Gina was sitting on the porch with the other victims.  There were psychologists on the way for the counseling these ladies would need after their ordeal, but she had to take their official statements. Many of the women were crying, and Gina was kind enough to put an arm around them to comfort the ones who needed it the most.  Daphne wasn't an expert on human psychology, but she knew enough to know this would affect them all for the rest of their lives.

"My Gracie saved us, didn't she?" Mrs. Collins said up to Daphne as she approached the group of women.

"She did.  And she's with you now," Daphne explained.  Once the cops had arrived, Grace had gone to her mother's side and never left.

"I know."  Through a tearstained face, Mrs. Collins smiled.  "When they kidnapped me, she tried to warn me.  I just didn't understand."

"How could you have possibly known the people who killed your daughter would want you too?" Daphne asked, her arms folded across her chest.  She meant it in a supportive way, but it didn't completely sound kindhearted even to her own ears.

"But you understand her.  And see her."  It wasn't a question.  She seemed to accept Daphne's ability with open-mindedness.  Of course, she had seen it all first-hand a couple of times tonight.

Daphne nodded. "I'm a psychic medium. I help the police solve crimes." Daphne looked at Gina, realizing that she had been a bit presumptuous. She had been on payroll with the LAPD, but this case had just been a random thing with the Fresno PD.

But Gina smiled in return. "I know *I've* loved having you on the case."

Daphne couldn't help it. She smiled a bit in return. Yes, she had strong feelings for Miguel, one might even say she loved him. She didn't know—she'd never loved anyone before. But she was also finding she loved her new life here in Fresno. She felt something weird taking her over. It was a sense of belonging. And she liked it. After a lifetime of being the weirdo and freak, she was accepted—and even liked—for who she was.

"It's time," Grace said softly to Daphne. There was a sense of peace washing over her and Daphne understood what she was trying to say. Daphne had seen it hundreds of times in her lifetime. Grace was ready to crossover now and needed Daphne to explain it to her mother.

"Mrs. Collins."  Daphne started to reach for the woman who had endured so much these past few days, but then she thought better of it and pulled her hands back.  "Grace's work here is finished.  It's time for her soul to be at peace."

Mrs. Collins surprised Daphne by grabbing her hands and squeezing them, her eyes brimming with tears. "I know.  And it's okay.  Just tell her to visit me every now and again."

Daphne looked at Grace, who nodded in return, a huge smile filling her beautiful face.  A golden light surrounded her, backlighting her.  She looked just like an angel standing there on the front porch of the home where so many people's lives had been ruined.

"Thank you, Daphne."

"Thank you, Grace.  Rest in peace."

And the light surrounding Grace got brighter at first and then slowly faded from view. The connection to her soul was a tangible thing to Daphne.  She could feel it the minute it was gone, like an actual rope slipping from her fingertips. "She's gone."

She wasn't exactly sure what emotional state Mrs. Collins would be in, so she continued holding her hands. But Mrs. Collins was surprisingly calm. Letting Daphne's hands go, she turned to the other victims. "My Grace's our hero." Daphne suspected this story would become legend—the murder victim whose ghost saved so many others from the same fate.

Good.

Gina stood to match Daphne, brushing her slacks as she stood. She looked like she was about to say something when Officer Long came out the front door.

"We hit the motherload, Detective. Turns out Ronnie Blackwood kept a journal, detailing everything. We found the gun that was used to shoot Miguel, too."

"I hope Judge Bustamante's fingerprints are all over that sucker," Gina said, shaking her head.

"He's mentioned by name throughout the journal," Officer Long explained. "My guess is the Judge had no idea that Ronnie was logging everything or he would've taken care of it years ago."

Gina stole a glance at the eight victims they had saved from the crime ring. "Well, we can't help the ones we lost, but we can get them all justice. Let's make sure we hand an airtight case to the prosecution so those bastards get what's coming to them."

Officer Long nodded. "I just can't believe Judge Bustamante was the one running all this for all these years. He's killed or trafficked hundreds of girls."

"Well, I'm no expert on people," Daphne interjected, "but I know that some people just can't ever get enough. Never enough power, never enough money, never enough sex. It's probably why he was so fat." Daphne frowned but was surprised when Gina laughed.

"You always say you don't understand people, but yet you seem to know us all better than we know ourselves." Gina put a kind hand around Daphne's shoulders and squeezed. It was loving and supportive. "Now are you ready to give me your sworn statement?

You *are* our star witness."

Oh, yeah. Daphne had forgotten that she wasn't technically working this case. "Well, when we got here, Miguel heard a familiar voice and he wanted to follow it but I wanted to stay focused on rescuing the girls. So we parted ways."

Gina pulled out a notebook and jotted down some notes before looking up at Daphne. The porchlight was on now and it cast a halo around Daphne that made her look magical standing there in front of the old Victorian home on a moonless night.

"Speaking of which, how did you subdue two guards all by yourself? And where did you learn to tie knots like that?"

"Oh. Grace helped me. Like Mrs. Collins said, she's a hero."

Gina tightened her lips in thought. "We may have to fudge that one a little bit in the official report."

"She helped with the Judge too. When I heard the gunshot, I ran to help Miguel and make sure he was okay.  I left the girls, I'm sorry to say, but my mind was on Miguel's safety."

Gina nodded.  She understood.

Daphne continued.  "On my way up the stairs I ran into the cowardly Judge trying to sneak off in the middle of the night.  Grace made sure he didn't leave until you arrived."

"Do I dare ask how she did that?"

"She held him up against the wall."

Gina whistled.  "That can't have been easy.  He's a big guy."

Daphne rolled her eyes.  "It's easy for a ghost with pent up anger and frustration.  It's like when Popeye eats his spinach."

Gina smiled.  She genuinely liked Daphne's brusque manner.  "Well, I like that between your story, Miguel's and the paper trail upstairs, Judge Bustamante is going to get what's coming to him. We can probably get Ronnie Blackwood to turn on him to save his own bacon."

"So, Ronnie gets off easy?"

"Well, the goal is usually to bring down the crime boss.  We'll keep an eye on Ronnie to make sure he doesn't pick everything back up again when he gets out, but good chance he was just doing what he was told the whole time anyway.  He'll be lost without the Judge.  He's not a mastermind."  At Daphne's frown she placed a gentle hand on Daphne's forearm.  "Don't worry. Rick the murderer will pay fully for his murders."

Daphne snorted.  "Oh, that guy's going to get prison justice."

Gina laughed out loud.  "He was still pretty shaken up by being tormented by the ghost of one of his victims, let me tell you.  It was way more a punishment than the law could ever give.  He'll probably be mumbling incoherently in a jail cell for years to come."

"Good.  Guys like that always think they can play God, taking lives at will.  A little dose of the reality in exactly how big this universe really is will do him some good."  Daphne looked at Gina, straight in the eyes. "I play a very small role in all of this, but getting justice for the dead?  That's my purpose on this Earth."

"I know."  Gina hugged Daphne's shoulders.  "I'm glad Miguel found you.  I think you're really going to ground him."  Daphne didn't know what to say to that, so she just stood there silently with Gina's arm draped across her shoulders, trying hard to pretend this was something that happened to her every day.  "Welcome to the team, Daphne.  I look forward to many more opportunities to get justice for the dead with you."

# 25.

Mrs. Collins found herself staring out the window, seeing but not registering anything her eyes were taking in.  Her thoughts were frozen to a place in history where a young Grace Collins was riding her bike in the street in front of the house.  Mrs. Collins watched as her little girl pedaled as fast as she could, taking wide turns when she wanted to circle back, her blonde ponytails moving with the breeze.

When she peered into the past with her memories, Mrs. Collins found that she could be happy again.  It was almost like playing pretend.  Pretend the good ole days were still happening.  Pretend that nothing bad ever happened in this world.  Pretend Grace was still alive and playing in the front yard. Even if just for a stolen moment or two, it provided a reprieve from the harsh realities of the life that Mrs. Collins was actually living.

Distantly, she thought she might have heard a soft knocking on a door somewhere. She ignored it. She just needed a few more minutes watching her baby play.

When the doorbell rang, she snapped from her memory and was thrust squarely into the here and now. Someone was at the door. Mrs. Collins sighed. Good chance it was reporters. They all wanted her story now, and while it was exhausting, Mrs. Collins enjoyed the opportunity to keep Grace's memory strong in the press.

It wasn't her dream for the day, but Mrs. Collins knew that one day no one would care anymore. So she didn't want to miss one single story. Steeling herself for the interview, she opened the door.

And she startled a bit when she realized it was Ellie who stood before her.

The smile was forced, but Ellie did it anyway. Her

face was still bruised, and she looked frail—as if she'd lost 20 pounds she never had to lose in the first place.  She was holding a small pot.  "Hi, Mrs. Collins."

"I thought you were a reporter," Mrs. Collins said by way of greeting.

Ellie nodded.  "They won't leave me alone either."

"Do you want to come in?"

"I just…" Ellie started, lifting the pot she was holding.  "I was planning to plant this.  In memory of Grace.  And, well…I thought maybe you'd like to plant it with me."

"Oh."  Mrs. Collins frowned, despite the rational thought that she was being rude.  What a tangible reminder of the fact Grace was truly gone.  But she forced herself to smile, although it wasn't very warm or meaningful—a lady could only fake so much—because she knew Ellie was also grieving and was also a victim.  "What is it we're planting?"

"A calla lily," Ellie explained.

Mrs. Collins leaned over and saw a small twirl of a leaf popping through the soil. With very little expression supporting her words, she responded, "That sounds lovely." She stepped out onto the front porch with Ellie, closing the door behind her. Wordlessly, she walked toward a small brown chest nestled on the side of the house between two bushes.

She lifted the lid and pulled out a small hand trowel and two pairs of gloves. "Where shall we plant it?"

Ellie shrugged. "I didn't really plan that far ahead."

Placing a gentle hand on Ellie's wrist, Mrs. Collins nodded toward the driveway. "I think I know a place." She walked toward a flowerbed which lined the driveway. There was an area where steppingstones connected the grass to the cement. Mrs. Collins lifted the stones and set them aside, creating a wide space for a new plant. "This is where I watched Grace run many times. To get her bike. To climb in my car. The first day of school. Prom. She crossed this very path often."

Tears welled in her eyes at the memory and Ellie felt herself being caught up in the emotion. Ellie swallowed and responded. "It's perfect."

The two ladies knelt on the grass as they dug a small hole in the dirt and placed the young calla lily in it. As they worked, a bright yellow butterfly kept fluttering around them.

"That's interesting," Ellie commented.

"Hmmm?"

"That butterfly. I saw it at my house too, I think. It's such an unusual color—that's how I recognized it," Ellie explained.

"It's Grace," Mrs. Collins said. This time when she smiled, she actually meant it. She could feel Grace near and it brightened up her soul one tiny piece at a time.

"Grace," Ellie whispered as she stretched out a hand to let the butterfly land. She had never thought that a butterfly could be her friend's soul, but after the experience she'd had in the warehouse, she wasn't one to dispel it, either.

"I think she's happy with your idea to plant this," Mrs. Collins said.

The butterfly finally stopped fluttering and stayed on Ellie's hand.  "I hope so."  She pulled her hand a bit closer to her chest.  "The psychic said that I had survivor's guilt."

"I think I do, too.  How could we not?  We escaped when so many didn't."

"Do you know what's funny?" Ellie continued, watching the yellow butterfly as it stayed on her hand. "When I was first out of the hospital, I was bursting to tell Grace my whole ordeal.  I started to call her.  I was so caught up in my own trauma, I forgot all about what happened to Grace. I forgot she was gone."

Mrs. Collins put an arm around Ellie's shoulder. "I think you can talk to her whenever you want to.  And what's even better is you don't need a device to do it. Tell her whatever you want."  Mrs. Collins looked back out into the street where minutes before she had been lost in a memory.  "I always do."

"I miss you, Grace," Ellie whispered to the butterfly.  At her words, the butterfly flew from her hand, circled their heads and flew into the afternoon sky.  Both ladies watched it until they could no longer see the yellow wings.

They sat in silence, the twirling leaf of the budding calla lily before them.  Mrs. Collins thought about how much this had meant to her.  Sitting next to her was a young woman who had been through the same thing she had.  Not very many people could understand.  Her husband was going through his own stages of grief, and he didn't appreciate when she opened up about her own, since it effectively laid it on him.  Her friends were sympathetic but had no way of understanding the depth of emotions.

But Ellie did.

"Thank you for this.  It was a truly lovely idea," Mrs. Collins told Ellie, indicating the plant before them.  But she meant it for so much more. The plant was a nice gesture and a pleasant, tangible reminder of Grace's life, but also just having Ellie think of her and be there with her was soothing for her soul.

Ellie rested her head on Mrs. Collins's shoulder, enjoying the comfort from the mother figure.

They were far from healed, but a little warm spot had developed in both their hearts and they could feel it melting some of the pain and darkness.

They sat there together, watching the calla lily bud nestled in the ground and enjoying the tiniest feeling of peace amongst all the swirling thoughts and feelings of horror, fear, pain and loss.

# 26.

A week later and Daphne ran to the front door to let Miguel into her tiny apartment.  His arm was still bandaged and in a sling, but it was healing well.  He would make a full recovery.  Daphne had been going to his place the last few nights since he'd left the hospital, because driving was hard for him.  But today he was excited to come to her since his shoulder had healed enough that he felt capable of driving again.

When she opened the door, she smiled warmly at the sight before her.  He was dressed casually by Miguel's standards, but he still looked clean cut and handsome in a white button-up shirt and jeans.  His hair was perfectly gelled in place and he smelled wonderfully of some pleasant aftershave.

Daphne, by contrast, was her usual disheveled self.  She had on a long black skirt and nothing on her bare feet.  Her blonde hair stuck up in every direction.  Her make-up raccooned underneath her eye.  And she didn't care one bit.  Miguel didn't seem to, either, and it was one of the things she really liked about him.

Before she could stop herself, she jumped up on Miguel and kissed him. It was just an instinct of pure happiness at seeing him.  But he groaned and gently pushed her off of him.

"My shoulder, Daph."

"Oh, yeah.  Sorry."

He cupped her chin with his good hand.  "Promise me you'll try that welcome again when my wound is healed."

She stepped up on her tippy toes and placed a gentle kiss on his cheek.  "Come in."  She held the door open as he entered her apartment living room and made himself at home in one of her chairs.  Her apartment was minimalistic.  Not much adorned the walls and not much furniture filled the space.  But there was a photograph with a certain prominence on the end table near Miguel's seat.

On instinct, he picked it up and looked at the faces smiling around Daphne.  She wasn't smiling in the picture, neither was a bald man covered in tattoos who stood with his arms folded, but the other three in the photograph had huge grins.

"Family?" Miguel asked her.

Daphne sat on the armrest of Miguel's chair. "Basically, but not by blood."  She pointed at the large man in the middle.  "This is Duncan.  He started the Paranormal Investigators League and occasionally asks me to help him on cases.  He's the closest thing to a brother I've got."

Miguel put the framed photograph back.  "You're not close to your real family?"

"More like they're not close to me," Daphne explained.  There was no sadness in her voice.  She'd gotten so used to being an outcast that rejection meant very little to her anymore.  Not everyone accepted her for who she was, and she was fine with that.  "People in my family got tired of my quirks, as they called it.  And I got tired of trying to be something I wasn't to make people happy.  It's exhausting."

"My family wanted me to be a lawyer," Miguel said.

"I know."  Daphne smiled.

"Are you always going to know everything about me before I tell you?"

Daphne shrugged.  "I can always fake like I don't."

Miguel squeezed her hand.  "You know you don't ever have to lie or be fake around me.  Just takes some getting used to, that's all.  It's a trip how you talk to ghosts."

Daphne looked at the floor.  She didn't really know what to say.  Talking to ghosts was as normal as breathing for her.

Miguel tipped her chin to force her to look into

his eyes.  "But it's also super cool. You saved a lot of people.  There's no way Gina and I would've solved this case as quickly without you."

"You would've eventually figured it out."  Daphne climbed onto Miguel's lap, carefully making sure to avoid his wounded shoulder this time.  "But I have to say, you really needed Grace."

"Yeah, I guess I did."  Miguel wrapped his good arm around Daphne's waist, holding her tight.  "And I believe in ghosts now, so there's that."

Daphne shook her head.  "People always announce their belief or disbelief like it matters. Whether you believe or not doesn't make it any less true."

He laughed and squeezed her tighter.  "Well, I suppose I should've said, I'm more open to listening to the victims in my cases."

Daphne thought of Maddy, an image of a little girl with crooked pigtails flashed in her mind.  "Yeah. They've probably been screaming at you for years."

"Do you know what I first thought about you when you contacted me early in the case saying you had information from the victim?"

Daphne snorted. "Yeah. You thought I was crazy. Everyone does.  That's why I gave you Cayman's number."

Miguel smiled.  "After that."  He shook his head at the memory of calling her crazy-lady-on-line-two.  "I thought you were relentless.  You never gave up and I admired that. I still do."

Daphne smiled at the validation.  She may not be Miss Congeniality, but she did pride herself on bulldozing through people's bullshit.

Miguel sighed as he switched back to the topic he knew was on both their minds. "Kevin Kyle turned on Rick Bersin.  Rick's going to take the full fall and Kevin will get a reduced sentence for testifying.  I thought you might like to know that, if you don't already."

"Have all the victims' families been notified?"

Daphne thought about all the women over the

years, lost, sold or dead.  So many families with no closure.  Daphne was all about closure.  There were a lot of things we could take as human beings if we had the information and the time to process it.  But not knowing?  That's the edge of reason and madness.

The wondering, hoping, filling in blanks with your own imagination, that's where people began to spiral into dark pits with no escape.

"Not all of them yet.  Spencer is still tracking many of them down.  There were a lot."  Miguel cleared his throat to hide the bit of emotion that had snuck its way in.  "Speaking of Spencer, he found a very obscure paper trail connecting Judge Bustamante to The Born Stars.  There are so many deaths and kidnappings associated with his name, I don't know if he'll ever leave his cell.  No parole for the crooked ole judge."

"So Gina's been giving you updates?" Daphne asked.

"You know it.  She knows I'd be going crazy sitting at home without knowing what was happening on my case."

"I'm glad Grace and all those girls are getting the justice they deserve. I hate it when evil wins."

Miguel shifted a bit so he could get a better look at Daphne. "Did you know that they were planning to sell Mrs. Collins to a Prince? I guess he requested a mature woman to act as his 'head of staff' for his servants. He was obsessed with old literature where a matronly woman always ran the household."

Daphne wrinkled her face in pure disgust. "And he couldn't find any of his own people? It had to be some random lady from Fresno?"

"The Judge had some far-reaching connections, I guess. And Mrs. Collins was easy prey they already knew about."

"Assholes." Daphne looked at her hands, her mind seeing the spiritual world all around her. "There's a big difference, you know. Between violent deaths and natural ones. Difference in the souls, I mean."

"I can imagine."

"I prefer the peaceful souls. They're usually lost and confused, but when your life's been stolen from you... There's no peace when they come to me." Again Daphne saw Maddy. Without her murderer behind bars, Maddy's soul would never rest. And neither would Daphne.

Suddenly Daphne stood up, an idea coming to her. "How much time do you have off?"

"Two weeks while my arm recovers. In case you didn't notice, I took a bullet from a perp." He smiled a cocky smile that showed how secretly proud he was of his bullet wound.

"That might be enough," Daphne said to herself.

Miguel stood up next to her. "Enough for what?"

Daphne flashed a mischievous smile. "Wanna come with me to Southern California and solve the cold case of Madison Laurens?"

Miguel widened his eyes in shock. "Work on the LAPD's case? I don't think so."

Daphne made a face. "It's no one's case, believe

me.  If Cayman couldn't solve it, no one in the LAPD is going to fight for it.  It's just sitting on ice."  She grabbed Miguel's hands.  "And we make a great team."

The wheels were spinning inside Miguel's head.  He could stay here for two weeks going stir crazy in his apartment not doing anything.  Or they could take a road trip and he could help Daphne with the case that got away.  "Will we bring Cayman into our little investigation?"

Daphne shrugged.  "If you want.  I know this case haunts him too."

"I have cases that haunt me too, so I get it.  I'll come with you on one condition," Miguel stated, but Daphne was already bouncing on her bare feet with joy.  "We're not doing this as co-workers."

Daphne cocked her head to the side.  She wasn't used to so completely failing to understand Miguel's thoughts and emotions.  "I don't get it."

He smiled at Daphne and she felt weak at the sight of it.  "You introduce me to Cayman as your significant other."

Daphne rolled her eyes. "You made it seem like it was some big thing. You're my soul mate. I'd go as a husband-and-wife team if I didn't think it would freak you out."

Miguel stepped a bit closer to Daphne. "It doesn't." And weirdly, he found that despite only knowing her a week or so, marrying her didn't weird him out at all. Every other relationship in his past terrified him when he thought about marriage. What was it about this quirky blonde psychic?

He was inches from her face and looking at her with complete adoration. No one had ever looked at her that way before. His face, his smile, his scent. It was all so intoxicating.

"Your Tia Lencha said she's proud of you and she can admit she was wrong. She thinks you're a better cop than you would've been a lawyer." Daphne wrapped her arms around Miguel's neck and pulled him closer.

"Is she here now?" Miguel looked around,

slightly uncomfortable.

Daphne shook her head. "She came to me in a dream the other night."

"Good.  Because if ghosts are going to be popping up every time I want to kiss you, this relationship is going to really test my manhood.  I can't perform with ghosts watching."

"You get used to it."  And she pulled Miguel in, closing what little distance there was between them, and kissed him with everything she had in her heart.

And it felt like home.

Without pulling away she asked, "So when do we leave for SoCal?"

To be continued in the Daphne Winters Book Two:

*Finding Maddy*